BONES &
BLOOD

Bones & Blood

Out for Blood #1

K. B. Thorne

For news about new releases, exclusive extras, and promotions, sign up for my newsletter at my website!

K. B. Thorne, Author of Sci-fi & Fantasy
http://authorkbthorne.com

Dedicated to Monica Hay and all the lovely people at the Writer's Way Membership who have helped me find my way back. Like a vampire, my gratitude is eternal.

A Little Backstory

This is the first book in its series, but it is also a sequel to my nine-book Blood Rights Series. You should not need to read the first series to get into this one, but I'm going to write a small primer on the world here for those who haven't.

The Blood Rights and Out for Blood Series take place in a sort of alternate universe. It is basically our modern world in the United States, but there was one major divergence in 2009 when Cameron St. John and Sadie Stanton—a werewolf and a vampire, respectively—stepped forward to propose a wild, dangerous concept.

They suggested that all preternatural beings should be recognized as not only real but as legal beings.

This began a long—and ultimately fatal—fight for preternatural rights that saw discussions, debates, scientific and medical studies, committees, and protests that led to the passing of the Preternatural Rights Act of 2010...or, more commonly, Cameron's Law. It was named for Cameron St. John, who was murdered by an anti-preternatural hate group just before it was signed into law.

Sadie Stanton, the survivor of the pair, lives in Adelheid, CT, and runs the Stanton Agency. This business helps the preternatural but also helps the human populace with the preternatural. The city of Adelheid has become something of a hotspot for vampires, werewolves, and more as the U.S. has moved from the new law to many new ways of existing.

Even if much in this world is just the same as the real world and hasn't diverged too far, it is still an alternate reality and so some details of their 2010 and onward will have been and will be different than ours.

If you want to know more, I invite you to check out my series wiki, which has information about the city of Adelheid and its history, the Blood Rights Series and its characters, the Stanton Agency, the Preternatural Rights Act of 2010, and a guide to the preternatural that discusses the lore I chose to use for the books:

wiki.authorkbthorne.com

Author's Note

I wrote the last story in the Blood Rights Series—*Flesh & Blood*—in 2016, though I said it wasn't going to be a total end. I didn't know if I'd ever go back to modern Adelheid, however. I had, and still have, ideas for different series based off the characters but taking place in different timelines and settings.

Those didn't happen, though. Not yet, at least.

There's been a long span now where I have struggled with writer's block. Most of what I've managed to write has been for the charity anthologies that I've put together or co-written works. I enjoyed all those stories and I'm proud of them, but it's still not the same as putting together work that's *just* mine.

I got a huge helping hand up, however, when I attended Monica Hay's "Overcoming Writer's Resistance Bootcamp" and then became part of her Writer's Way Membership. (I can't shout her out enough, by the way. I'm sorry. I've become an acolyte.) If you're having a tough time, I recommend looking her up at monicahaycoaching.com.

Anyway. When I turned back to my own work, I decided that I needed to go back to the beginning. That's Adelheid. I started writing for Sadie and Dakota when I was still a teenager. (I won't tell you how long, but that was a long time ago.) My fictional world has changed a lot as I matured creatively, but the soul of the characters remains.

And as much as I love Sadie, Dakota has kind of always been my favorite.

My mother has told me that Dakota is me if I "said everything I thought." That's really rather true. I wish I could just, you know, hiss like a rattlesnake at people who annoy me, but I don't. One, I'm more polite than that. Two, I can't shapeshift my vocal cords. I won't rule out that if I *could* shapeshift my vocal cords, I might in turn be less polite.

But I digress.

So, we popped ahead a few years from *Flesh & Blood* to *Bones & Blood*, which is the first of the Out for Blood books and will feature Dakota as the only narrator. This is a big departure from the Blood Rights stories, which feature different narrators for each one. A couple narrators repeated, but there were many voices for Blood Rights.

Out for Blood is just Dakota. The cast from the first series is all present and will be active participants in the stories, but they won't be the storytellers this time.

I hope that you'll enjoy living in Dakota's head as much as I do, for this story and many others to come.

Thank you and enjoy!

K. B. Thorne
August 2025

CHAPTER ONE

One lesson I've learned during my absurdly long life is that the past repeats itself in varying ways.

Next is that if you don't learn from it, you're doomed to be screwed by it.

Coming in third is that you shouldn't be a jackass to the people who care about you...which is a continual work-in-progress for me.

And my fourth incontrovertible truth is that every forest in New England is pretty similar to every other forest in New England, and despite the effort of human 'progress,' there are still a lot of forests. Even so, every area has its own feeling and its own scent. I could never mistake being in a forest in southern Maine for being in a forest of northern Connecticut.

Who am I, and why do I know the intricacies of forests so well? My name is Dakota, and I've spent a lot of time hunting out in the wooded lands.

At that precise moment, I was rushing through one such forest, surrounded by the autumn foliage that lured a stupid number of visitors to this area every year. I had taken on a pretty basic job of hunting a vampire bail-jumper. The crime was low-rent compared to the criminals I usually pursued in my job as a preternatural bounty hunter, all things being equal. Aggravated assault after he and a pyrokinetic got into a drunken bar brawl. Vampires could go up in flames like kindling, which was the only way it was any sort of real fight, since a vampire has far superior strength to any human. The pyro part of that human gave them a one-up, but it wasn't enough to avoid getting knocked around.

The penalty probably would've been minimal, if anything, since the bar was full of witnesses to say that both people had been equal participants and the pyro even started it, but the vampire was young and had done a dumb. Becoming an eternal creature of the night did not equal a suddenly smart creature. He got bailed out then took off.

I didn't happen to have anything else going on about that time and got fidgety if I had to stay in the house for too long a stretch, so it seemed like a good way to pep things up. I mean, I loved my brother— even if I very rarely admitted it out loud—and I did like his wife. I loved my girlfriend, too, but she had to work a lot. Cop hours and all that. I loved my dog... but I thought he even got tired of me once I started getting restless. Then there were all the other dogs on the property who barked *a lot.*

Anyway. So. I was running through the forest, hell bent for lecture, in the body of a mountain lion because that was the form I liked the best. Each of us—my family, when they were all alive—had our preferences, though back in the days when we were young, we had to be far more careful about shapeshifting than I did now. The freedom of legality was pretty fucking fantastic, although some of the scare factor had been reduced as people got used to us.

Having four legs made for a much better running speed, but vampires could reach inhuman velocity with just two. I wasn't sure how it worked but something about the dark magic that animated the whole species after death gave them a lot of perks. Biologists since legalization had made many strides in understanding the different science behind the preternaturals, but vampires were still proving the hardest nuts to crack, so to speak.

I heard a branch break and then saw the leaves of a tree not far ahead start to shake as if being rattled by a really big squirrel. If my feline lips could have smirked, they would have, because I knew he had just climbed a tree.

Did he think that would help him get away? Ridiculous.

I leapt and leapt high. Even "normal" mountain lions could leap over thirty feet, and I had the benefit of not needing to let my feet touch down again. As I reached the height of my arc, I shifted. Theriomorphs don't have to go through all that extra time and messy clothing splits and painful bone cracks like other shapeshifters. We just...change. I was a lion and then I was a bird, winging my way through the branches and homing in on my target. It was a transition I had made hundreds of times, so my brain's wiring did fine to move me from four-legged sprints to two-winged flight.

I screamed, avian-style.

The vampire ahead, leaping from branch to

branch, turned to look over his shoulder in alarm. In his haste, he lost his balance and fell to the ground. I folded my wings against my body and dove after him. My talons latched onto his shirt just as he was getting to his feet, and in a truly graceless display for a species stereotyped for their elegance, he flailed and screamed like a three-year-old.

My nails dug in, getting past the shifting fabric of his clothes and into the meat of his shoulder. It wasn't like blood loss would be an issue, but vampires still felt pain. The screaming intensified, and I almost let go because the sound was so incredibly painful on my supercharged hearing.

Still whirling and swatting at me, he started to run again. Or it was kind of like running. I'm not really sure what the right word was for this gait, but he did it. Eventually, he'd tire. Vampires had their own version of running out of stamina.

I had time, just as long as I spent less energy than he did.

The angle did not allow him to get both hands on me, and his panicking hands did not even let one get a good grip on my feathers. Really, if he would just have stopped moving and thought it through for a moment, he probably would've been able to tear me off. Yeah, he'd lose some flesh, but my claws weren't silver. He would grow it back. But he was pretty new as a vampire, if I recalled right, so he was not fully aware of the extent of his abilities now that he was a part of the graveyard group.

As distracted as I was by his strange gyrations, I did not notice that we were closing in on a ramshackle, abandoned house in the middle of some half-cleared woods. When I finally caught sight of it, my brain tried to fill in the gaps from the momentary glimpse. My brain said...1800? Used to be farmland but there was a second growth forest half-grown around it.

We went barreling through the door, breaking it down.

Rude, I thought.

If all of this hadn't been weird enough, right? It was about to get weirder.

As it turned out, the house wasn't actually abandoned. From the outside, it looked like there couldn't possibly be any living things inside and... Well, technically that was true, because there weren't any *living* things in the house. There were vampires. There was a fuck-ton of vampires. While I still don't really know the weight difference between a ton and a fuck-ton, the latter seemed to be the most accurate measurement of what I found.

I let go of the kid's shoulder just before he gracelessly crashed through a rotted floorboard, flying a few feet over to a section of floor with a disgusting chair on it. I didn't like the furniture, but I figured if there was a chair, the floor under it was more solid than the part the young guy had just gone through. I landed on the seat and then waited a moment to see if I was about to plummet to the root cellar. When nothing happened, I took a breath for a sigh of relief and immediately regretted it.

Remember when I said there were a ton of vampires? Well, something that humans don't know is that vampires smell weird. Mind, not even all preternatural species have heightened senses of smell at the same level of intensity. I had spent so many decades of my life as an animal that smell was one of my top senses. And vampires smelled like graveyard dirt. It was generally faint if there was just one of them, or they were really young, but when there was a whole room/house full of various ages? That was another matter altogether.

It's also important to note that they do not smell of decay, exactly. They are undead, so they don't rot. It's more the sense of the graveyard, not of a corpse, but that's a distinction that is always hard to explain.

Anyway, the house reeked of them, and I wondered if they'd all been in here for a long time... which also would have been weird. Vampires didn't need hidden protective nests anymore...

However, I didn't have a lot of time to think about that right then.

It was clear none of them had expected visitors or even their fellow vamp. About seven or eight sitting in the room ahead of me just stared in shock. There was a large bird of prey hanging out on the living room décor and a big hole in the floor, neither of which having been there before.

This felt like a situation that was going to bear a little explanation since I still had to grab the kid before I left and I didn't want a fight on my hands. I could probably escape alive, but seven vampires and one me were still pretty shitty on the odds.

So, as politely as one could do such a thing, I shifted from bird back to human. My magic was far happier than any of your standard were-creature because my magic kept my clothes with me.

Anything I touched was wrapped up in it, so none of the Incredible Hulk torn wardrobe shit like the werewolves and such had to deal with if they shifted on the spur of the moment.

I expected some surprise, but it was usually less surprising for other preternatural creatures to see a shapeshifter because we were all part of the big magical weirdo family, right? Not so, as it turned out, for this crowd. I shifted fluidly into my human form, held up a hand, and opened my mouth to speak…

Someone else's scream came out.

I was shocked right back into silence when the whole bunch of them lost their ever-loving minds. I hadn't had anything like this happen since the one time I accidentally surprised a very large group of under-initiated humans in the middle of a shopping mall, but vampires weren't usually this easy to spook. But spook, they did.

I thought I made out an exclamation of "what do you want" from one of them, but most just scattered down halls or through doors, and one even went out the window.

I knew I wasn't the most social of creatures, but people usually didn't do this just at the sight of me.

"I just want the kid in the basement," I called over the noise, still perplexed as hell.

One vampire who hadn't fully fled the room yet—a woman—dove through the hole in the floor. A moment later, she leapt right back into the room. Vampires could do wild acrobatics like that. They couldn't actually fly or anything, but they could definitely jump higher and further than any human could. She also had my target vamp in her hands and shoved him right toward me.

For a person who doesn't shock very easily, I was hitting three-for-three on surprises. Vampires usually didn't give each other up that quickly either, but it was obviously happening as the kid went stumbling toward me after the elder vampires pushed him my way.

My shock made me embarrassingly slow, and he managed to scramble to the side just before I got my hands on him. He took off right back out the door, and I was on his heels a moment later, leaving the mystery of the odd vampire nest behind me. I had to call it a nest rather than a coven house because of the abandoned, ratty-ass building they were all in.

Modern covens kept their stuff much nicer.

So, back out the door, but my quarry was on his heels now. There were big gashes in his shirt from where my bird claws had latched on, and he was obviously flabbergasted about what just happened. Had he known there were vampires in there and expected them to protect him? Or maybe he hadn't expected anyone and that alone had thrown him. Sure as hell had thrown me.

I lunged forward, two legs leaving the ground just before four of them landed on his back and drove him into the dirt.

I leaned down with my feline head and shrieked in his ear.

He shrieked right back.

Chapter Two

It was pretty much all over after that. He couldn't keep his shit together anymore, and I was able to get some of my custom-made zip ties around his wrists. A vampire would be able to bust out of any sort of old-fashioned ties or handcuffs, but mine were inscribed to prevent that. Once upon a time, I had faintly silver-threaded cuffs, but once the witches came up with these, I went for them as a little less nasty. I did have something of a heart in there somewhere, and he was hardly Al Capone. Mind, I wasn't happy about the merry little chase he had led me on, but I wasn't going to torture him for it.

The drive back to New London, CT—where he'd jumped bail—took about an hour, the way I drove. My catch, who was named Virgil Stokes, alternated between gibberish and silence. I wholeheartedly preferred the silence, even if it did give me time to think about how weird my evening had been. Why were vampires still congregating in shitty nests when they could live in the open or in coven houses? And what was with their reaction to me? And turning Virgil over to me like that... I appreciated that it made my job easier, but it was still fucking *weird*.

All these questions were giving me a headache, so I stopped thinking.

I turned him in at the police station, got my "job all done" slip, and then went home. It was pretty late by the time I got to our house, and I didn't want to wake anyone by tromping down the hallway, so I just crashed on the couch.

My hours could often be all-nighters, but Edward and Lorelei lived on a slightly more human timetable. They had to because of all the dogs our home/their dog rescue had that needed care. I helped here and there, but my main contributions were buying the house, property, and paying most of the bills.

I woke up however-many hours later to a tongue slobbering all over my face.

"What the—" I got out before the tongue went in my mouth and I sat up fast, hissing and spitting.

When I stopped, I looked down to see Buster staring up at me with that dopey grin pit bulls had on their blocky heads. He was the one living creature on earth that I could never seem to be mad at, though, even if he had just French kissed me. I vigorously pet his face in a way I swore I never would, and he just grinned bigger.

"Good morning, sunshine."

Okay, that wasn't the dog.

Standing in the door between the living room and kitchen was Detective Samantha Moore with a cup of coffee in her hand. The mug had a handle shaped like brass knuckles. It was my favorite.

"That for me?" I asked.

"Nope," she replied, then smirked. "But you can

have it anyway." She crossed to the couch and sat beside me, handing the mug over.

Sam was my girlfriend. Somehow. I still kind of couldn't believe that she was willing to put up with me, but here she was. She didn't actually live here, but she stayed over often enough that you just might think she did. I didn't mind. Which was also fucking weird. I'd gone from totally solo hermit to living with 2.5 other people and a dog inside plus a whole bunch more outside.

I still wasn't entirely sure how this had happened, yet I knew that I had completely done it to myself. I'd decided having my brother back in my life was the most important thing ever, and then it followed that I wanted his happiness, so I encouraged him to invite his girlfriend in Alabama to move up here, and she agreed. She hadn't wanted to leave her rescue work, though, so I facilitated their dream by using a big chunk of my long-term, hermit-life savings to buy a house with a huge plot of land to set up a dog rescue right here in Adelheid, CT. So that was all three of us together. I adopted Buster because I had somehow fallen in love with him, and I'd also somehow fallen in love with Sam, so here she was too.

I had no one to blame but myself, really.

Somehow, my brother and I had both fallen in love with humans, too. Also pretty fucking weird. Lot of fucking weird to go around. We kind of felt like we were robbing cradles, what with being four hundred, but Sam and Lorelei were totally adults so it wasn't like this was some terrible teen vampire romance or anything. Don't even start on that shit with me.

We both knew we'd watch our lovers die one

day...but we chose to pursue the relationships with humans anyway.

Love is fucking weird.

Anyways.

"Thanks," I mumbled as I took a long drink. I didn't even check how hot it was before I did so and discovered in an instant that it was pretty hot. It must have been fresh, given the way it sun-scorched my throat on the way down. I kind of didn't mind, though, because I...was a freak. Who knows why. "Eddie and Lorelei out with the dogs?"

"Of course," she said. "That latest batch from the hoarder house in Montville has made for a lot of last-minute work, so they've been out practically since the sun came up."

I squinted one eye and looked at her sidelong. "How long have you been here?"

She chuckled. "Since last night. I knew you'd be out on the hunt so I came over to keep Buster company until you got home." She looked down at his grinning face and scratched him behind the ears. Somehow, the smile got even bigger. I turned my side-eye to him, half-worried he was about to split his skull open at the corners of that grin.

"I'm sure he appreciates it," I said, turning back to the coffee. "I guess I do too."

Expressing any emotion other than anger or annoyance was not exactly my strong suit, but she really had to be used to that by now. After all, we'd been together for a couple of years now with just one intermission where she thought she couldn't stand me. I guess she got over it, and I was trying to behave less like a jackass.

"It's almost lunchtime now," she added, gesturing at the light as it came through the half-shut curtains over the living room window. I appreciated that no one had opened them completely on me. I wouldn't burst into flames like a vamp, but it would still get in the way of my sleeping. Maybe. Sometimes, I could sleep in broad daylight just fine. It seemed to depend on the day.

"Staying for food?" I asked, turning back to look at her.

She shook her head. "Afraid not. I've got plans to meet up with Nykk. I know it's my day off, but she's helping us with a witness in a case who is nearly incoherent and we're meeting for lunch to discuss it. This was the only time we both had free."

I realized I was a little disappointed. I kinda would have liked to have lunch with her, but I understood. Being a cop took up as much of one's time and energy—with just as much lack of care for the personal life—as my job did.

Nykk Marlowe used to be a cop. In fact, she used to have Sam's job as a detective with the Adelheid PD, but she'd left that job to become a victim's advocate. She still worked with the PD a lot but in a different capacity. I didn't see her much anymore, but by all accounts, she was really good at her job.

In that deep part of my brain where I wasn't a bitch, I did wish her well. Her road had been a hard one for a long time, but she seemed to be doing pretty good. She'd found her calling.

Not everyone was that lucky, I knew.

"I'll see you later?" Sam asked, bringing me back out of my half-asleep train of thought.

"Yeah," I said eloquently, nodding.

She kissed me, gave Buster another ear-scratch, and then left. I drank the rest of my coffee almost all at once and then left the mug on the table. I'd clean it up later. Probably. If Eddie didn't get to it first. Then, I moved to the bedroom.

It didn't take much to fall back asleep, even with the caffeine from the recently drunk coffee running through my system. That kind of thing doesn't last long in a preternatural body because our metabolism isn't like a human's. Things designed for human bodies tend to cycle faster out of ours. Fortunately, there was a whole market for items made for preter biology, but most of the stuff in the house—like food and drink—was the human kind since Lorelei and Sam were human. And frankly, us intaking human stuff had a less detrimental effect than humans taking stuff made for us. It was just one of those things.

I didn't really know how long I was able to stay asleep, however, before my brother and sister-in-law had finished with their tasks for the day. Or at least for the moment. They came inside with their house dogs, who made enough noise to get Buster riled up, and then he made enough noise to get me riled up.

I groaned and flopped onto my other side, dragging a pillow over my head to drown out the great variety of canine noises that were now taking place in sequence between the one inside my room and the ones outside my room. Chain barking. The struggle was real.

"Dude!" I finally exclaimed, tossing the pillow off my head and onto the floor. Buster jumped on it like he was going to attack it, but he was a good boy—despite the barking—and didn't actually do anything.

That was when I looked around and realized that I had just thrown my only pillow onto the floor, rendering it the sole property of Buster until I had the desire to go wrestle it away from him. I wasn't worried that I couldn't take him, of course, but still, I didn't really like taking things away from him. Naturally, this was a closely guarded secret of mine because I had a reputation to consider.

Grumpier now, I just yanked my blanket up toward my head and bundled it under my ear to go back to sleep. I did have the option to turn into a different creature that didn't like to have their heads on pillows so much, but I just didn't feel like it.

No one really knew what the "true" form of the theriomorph was supposed to be. If our parents were ever going to impart that knowledge on us, they both died in advance of actually doing so. We knew that we could take on almost any form that we wanted, only limited to certain biological organs across each form taken—that was, I would always have female organs even if could approximate outer male genitalia.

Anyway. My parents were both killed during a witch hunt back in 1628 when I was just fourteen, so certain information about our species had not been given to us. Furthermore, we had never met anyone else of our species. I didn't even know for sure if theriomorph was a good term, but it's what we ended up being called. The human form felt the most "natural" the majority of the time so I thought that was probably our origin form, but I could never be sure.

On the upside, I didn't have to melt into a bucket everyday like certain sci-fi characters one might know. I couldn't even turn to liquid. My forms were all bio-locked. All animals, in many forms, but nothing non-fauna, so to speak.

I just felt like staying in my human form right then, even if it wasn't as comfortable as another form might have been. I eventually did drift off into an irritable doze, and Buster joined me at some point that I couldn't remember.

At some other point further on, I was woken up again.

"Dakota!" my brother called, barging into my room.

"What the fuck!" I shouted. I pried one eye open to glare at his form vaguely silhouetted by the hallway lights. "What on earth do you want?"

"I just wanted to ask—"

"I don't care!" I shouted. "Ask me later when I've been allowed to wake up civilly!"

He didn't look impressed with my attitude, but being siblings for some-odd number of decades could do that to a couple of people. He was never impressed with my attitude no matter what I did. I even once put him in a headlock and dragged him around the house. I'd known, though, he was letting me because he changed to a smaller animal and skittered away when he'd decided he'd had enough.

Shapeshifter sibling fights are something else.

For the moment, he folded his arms over his chest and blew out an annoyed breath. "Whatever," he muttered, turning and leaving. He shut the door behind him, and I muttered myself back to sleep.

The next time I woke up, it was my own doing. I wasn't necessarily happy about it, because I'm not one of these people that are actually cheerful upon waking, but I was vaguely less grumpy because it hadn't been someone else's fault.

Buster jumped off the bed the moment my eyes opened, and I knew that he'd just been waiting for me. Since I was still mostly dressed, I rolled off the bed and onto the floor then I stood up. (Yes, that was how I did that. Don't judge me.) I half-staggered out of my room and into the hallway, seeing that the lights were off and the windows were dark. It was autumn, so it got dark early. It was probably around dinnertime now, if I had to guess. No one else was around, so I found my shoes and took Buster out.

We had a yard, but I liked to walk with him. It was literally impossible for him to get away from me, given the number of forms I had at my disposal to pursue him. Not that it even mattered since he never tried to get away. He wasn't as interested in the local small wildlife as some other dogs would be. He was so incredibly loyal and stuck right by my side whenever we went out together.

While we walked down the rural street, with its very sporadic streetlights, I texted with Sam a few times just to check in. I used to be pretty bad about that, but I'd gotten better since we got back together. See? You could teach a (really) old dog new tricks.

After the walk, I brought Buster back to the house. Brother and sister-in-law were still nowhere to be found, so I took care of things for my dog and then headed out.

I went to the office since it would probably be good to check in with the primary crew, i.e., those who worked the night shift.

As usual for a weeknight, Madison St. John was manning the front desk. She was a native New England werewolf who looked more like a cheerleader from Nebraska. Mind, she was definitely a case of looks being deceiving. I'd learned the hard way that she ran this office with an iron fist—or a furry claw, depending on how you wanted to look at it. I tried to find some of my own files once and had experienced a moment where I actually feared for my life, which was something that virtually never happened.

I'd gone up against preternatural nasties twice my size with less fear than I felt that day as I stared into the abyss of the Wrath of a Secretary.

"Good evening, Dakota," she greeted with her usual cheerful smile. "I have a note from the day admin that your last hunt was successful?"

"Yep," I agreed easily. My mind flashed back to the abandoned house in the middle of the woods and the apparent vampire nest, but I wasn't sure this was the time and place to bring it up. "Means I'm bored again, and we all know we don't want that. Anything new come in for me on the wire?"

Madison laughed. "The wire?"

I squinted at her. She laughed again but shrugged and didn't try to push the idea that my lingo and I were old-fashioned. We all already knew it. No need to keep saying it.

She handed me a small stack of papers, which I knew were messages that had been taken for me while I'd been out on the hunt. While having an office and a sort of "boss" to check in with, as well as Attila the Administrator in here, could be a little annoying at times, there were other times when it was kind of nice. Like having someone answer my calls and weed out the dumb messages from the useful ones.

I started flicking through them. Only a couple had any actual information about the potential job, and I usually took that to mean they weren't that interesting. I got a lot of calls for minor sorts of jobs, hunts that didn't require my level of skill, and they always tried to lure me in before actually giving me the information. Most of the time, I just ignored them. Every now and then, though, there was one worth following up. It was usually just a feeling about which ones were which.

Before I had a chance to decide, however, the phone rang. Madison answered it and then said, "Your timing is impeccable." She lifted the phone toward me. "It's Vance, and he needs to talk to you."

CHAPTER THREE

The police didn't call for my help very often, which really wasn't very surprising. They usually managed their own business, but every angle of law enforcement had gotten more complicated since preternatural legality. The infrastructure changes had been absurd, but the politicians got much happier and more cooperative when they realized that there was money to be made—more people living legal lives who had to pay taxes, and incentives and whatnot to cater to huge new populations and special interests and all that stuff that made me grumpy just to think about too much.

I wasn't a big fan of politicians.

Anyway, the department only called me when they had particularly tricky cases that somehow involved the paranormal. Vance and Sam were both preter themselves, of course, but I had more experience in certain areas. Like hunting things. Or, more importantly, like *catching* things.

"What can I help with?" I asked first thing as I walked into the precinct offices where my girlfriend and my boss's husband were sitting at their desks.

"Honestly, your greetings have gotten much

nicer since Sam has been beating you into shape," Vance deadpanned. "I must say that I like this far better than 'What the fuck do you guys want?'"

I made a face at him and an unpleasant animal noise then stood next to his desk with my arms folded across my chest, looking down at him judgmentally.

After a moment, I deadpanned back at him, "What the fuck do you guys want?"

He just smirked. I had clearly lost my edge with him. I'd have to work on that.

"Let's start with the background," Sam said, interrupting what might have escalated and gesturing to her computer monitor. "Watch this."

"I thought it was your day off," I commented.

She shrugged ruefully. "I'm not sure I know what a day off is anymore." She nodded back to the monitor.

I came around behind her chair. I didn't touch her or make any other show of affection because we were both on the job and total professionals. Or, really, she was. My little tete-a-tete with Vance probably showed otherwise in my case, but I'd do my best to behave now and not embarrass my girl in front of the boys. I'd only try to embarrass the boys.

There was a video already open on the screen, and she clicked play.

The room it showed was vaguely like an interrogation room but a little nicer, so I knew that this was some sort of witness and not a suspect. Human form, female, probably early to mid-twenties. Maybe a college student or close to it. And traumatized as hell. That was obvious from the way she sat. Her legs were pulled up on her chair, knees against her chest, arms around them as she watched everything with darting, wide-eyed movements.

Sam and Nykk were the ones talking to her.

The Sam at the desk and not on the screen spoke. "Twenty-three-year-old were-leopard," she explained. "Her name is Sarita Alvarez. Came into town just over three weeks ago to visit family after graduating college. She lives in Providence usually. She has family that's part of the wolf pack. Reported missing two weeks ago, about a week after she got here, and then was found three days ago. Last anyone knew, she'd been walking to Molly's diner but never arrived."

On the screen, "What can you tell us about what happened?" That was Nykk.

"Blue van," the girl said. "Blue. Big and blue. Grabbed me."

"Did you see anyone else in the van?" Sam asked gently.

The girl grunted. "No. Dark, everything dark. Sounds, other sounds."

I frowned slightly as I watched. I didn't usually talk to people who were caught in this kind of state. I was the first one to admit that putting me and traumatized people into the same room was usually a bad idea. It's not like I'd do anything on purpose, and I'd *try* to be nice, but I was not a gentle person. Everything about the way I looked and carried myself was purposefully to project the opposite effect. I was damn good at it, too.

"You were in town to visit your uncle?" Nykk tried a new tact.

"Yes. Yes. Uncle Jonah. Nice, always nice to me. Visiting from college. No. I'm out of college. Newly. Came to see him."

Before she said anything else about Uncle Jonah, she bounded out of the chair so fast that Sam and Nykk both jumped back. Sam was out of her seat in an instant, her hand hovering at her hip where she carried her service weapon, but she didn't pull it. She stood, frozen, watching the girl.

Nykk had remained in her seat, though she'd leaned back. They both watched the girl as she threw herself at the wall, banging it and acting like she was rattling bars.

"She was caged," I commented quietly.

"That was our thought too," the Sam here agreed, just as quietly. There wasn't really any reason for us to be quiet since the girl wasn't actually there with us, she was just on video, but it seemed more... respectful?

It took a couple minutes, but Nykk got her to calm down. She sat, but she didn't take the chair. She just sat with her back against the wall. "Blood and bones, blood and bones," she whispered.

"Blood and bones?" Nykk repeated carefully.

"Yes," the girl said, yipping like a puppy for a moment. That was particularly weird since she was a cat shifter. "Take your blood or break your bones."

She repeated that several times, and I tuned it out for a moment. "Where was she found?" I asked.

"Wandering down 395," Vance answered. "She was half-naked, but there wasn't any sign of sexual trauma. It looked more like the clothes had been torn, either by herself or maybe caught on something. She was badly injured. Some of it was silver infected and that made all her healing slow down."

One bit of lore that was true was about silver. It was a sort of paranormal allergy that every more-than-human creature was prone to. Human psychics seemed to have no problem, or so little problem as to not be noticed, but every vamp, shifter, demon, fae, or otherwise couldn't touch it. It messed with us in many different ways, and slowing down our innate fast healing was one of those ways, unfortunately. It was pretty shitty, too, though I had managed to dodge getting hit with silver for most of my time.

I knew others who hadn't, though, and it could scar even the likes of us. Nasty stuff. In her quieter moments, I could make out silver scars on this girl's face...

"They took her to the hospital, and it was clear that she'd endured some sort of torture, mental and physical, probably. She was a mess and referred to a center once her condition was stabilized. We were trying to interview her at the behavioral unit, but you can see that it wasn't easy."

I tuned back in on the screen when the girl made a sound reminiscent of a car backfiring or a gunshot, watching as Nykk and Sam did their best to try to get something, anything, out of the poor thing. "Killing fields," the girl whispered, turned back to the wall and scratching at it. But it was a sort of pathetic gesture, hopeless and feeble.

"She was only missing for not even two weeks?" I asked.

"Yeah," Vance said flatly. "By all accounts, she was a pretty happy and well-adjusted girl. This is a huge difference."

Even I felt my stomach turning. The mind could be broken way faster than any of us wanted to admit, but to go from "happy and well-adjusted" to this in not even two weeks... What sort of hell had she been put through in that time?

I didn't even want to try to imagine, though if was being called in, I was probably going to have to in order to do whatever it was they were asking me to do.

On the screen, the girl was making different noises. Some sounded like more gunshots while others were growls. "To the killing fields with him!" she whispered. "Blood and bones, Carson, blood and bones, the killing field, blood and bones, bones and blood..."

Sam turned the video off. There was discomfort in the air hanging over the three of us that even I could feel, and no one would ever call me the 'empathic' type. Truth be told, 'cement block' was more like the words usually thrown my way, and I was okay with that. I didn't really want to go around being touchy-feely with the world, but it was so thick for the group of us at that moment that no one could miss it.

After several taut moments, I cleared my throat slightly and asked, "So... What, ah, exactly is it that you would like from me?" The best way to get past an uncomfortable moment was to focus on the practical, I had always found.

"We obviously don't need you to find Miss

Alvarez," Vance said. It was kind of a stupid thing to say, but he probably was trying to sort out his thoughts the same way I was after what we'd just watched. "We would like to see if you can help us find where she was held, though. Our department is stretched pretty thin right now, and it's a pretty broad swath of territory that she may have been in. Plenty of deep forest and so on. It's hard to organize a force like ours to properly search all that when we're so light on help. You, on the other hand, have skills that we don't."

"Unending patience is not among them," I said with a half-smirk, but my heart wasn't in it. It was probably going to take a little while to regain my natural snark. "Give me what you got and I'll do what I can."

Sam smiled up at me gratefully. There was an edge to it that verged beyond the professional, but no one was going to comment on it. I acknowledged it with a very brief unprofessional expression of my own before I looked at her computer screen while she typed away on her keyboard.

"The doctors evaluated her injuries when we found her, giving us an idea of how far they think she could have made it while dealing with those and in the state of undress she was in—no shoes, for example—but also taking her species into account combined with the silver exposure. As we all know, shifters do slightly better than humans. Anyway, we've figured out this map," she said, pulling the image up, "of a radius around where she was found."

Vance got up from his own desk and came over to Sam's, gesturing at some red-shaded areas. "We've marked these off as having some element to the terrain that we don't think she could've gone through, either because of a physical impediment such as walking barefoot through a rock quarry with badly damaged feet or a busy area that she would have been seen passing through. Which we have no reports of."

I looked at the map. If she'd been human, this would have been easier. The big circle would have been a lot smaller. As it was, I could see their problem. It was still a big area to cover, and they couldn't be sure which direction she'd come in from to reach the point on I-395 where she had been found. That made possible locations in all four cardinal points, and quite a distance from each one.

"Can you give me a printout of this map?" I asked.

Sam's lips twitched. "So old-fashioned," she teased under her breath, although it wasn't like there was a preternatural in the room who couldn't hear her.

Vance chuckled. Our humor was returning. "That's what happens when you're older than dirt," he added. "On the upside, she's not asking for us to send her a message in smoke signals or hieroglyphics or something."

"You guys know that I'm standing right here, right?" I drawled.

"Of course," Sam said, pushing up from her desk and walking past me. "It would not be nearly as much fun if you weren't." Her hazel eyes flashed as she met my gaze, heading to the other side of the room where she pulled a piece of paper off the printer and brought it to us. She handed it to me. "Here you go."

"Thanks," I murmured, taking it and looking it

over. "Do you have any of the girl's personal effects? A scent would help."

"We have a couple things," Vance said. "Will you need to take it?"

I wanted to, but I also knew it was evidence. "Just a moment should be fine."

He nodded once and left the room, returning a minute later with a plastic bag. I took it, opened it, and inhaled deeply. It took a few breaths to catch her scent away from the dirt, but I got it. I handed it back and looked at Sam.

Her expression was somber again. "We appreciate all your help. If we can get a location, it should give us a leg up on figuring out what happened to her."

I nodded solemnly. "Like I said, I'll do what I—"

The phone on Sam's desk rang.

Chapter Four

Even though all the odds said that the call didn't have anything to do with me or the case of this girl, some strange little instinct told me to stay put for just a couple minutes longer. Vance went back to his desk as Sam stood next to hers to answer the phone. I leaned against the furniture while I waited, half-watching her from the corner of my eye while also trying to not be creepy and just stare at her while she spoke.

"Moore," she answered. She was silent for several long moments as she listened, but I could just make out the way her lips turned down and her brows knit. Her eyes flickered up to me, and I took that as a sign I could look directly at her. My instincts had been right, I was suddenly sure. She just made a few acknowledgement sounds before signing off.

"What was it?" I asked as she put the receiver back on the cradle.

"That was Nykk," she said.

I heard Vance shift in his seat behind me and knew we had his attention again. "What did she have to say? Was it about Alvarez?"

Sam pursed her lips slightly and nodded. "It

was," she said. "She said they were moving her between rooms and one of the orderlies, a vampire, happened to walk by. He didn't have anything to do with Miss Alvarez, but it was close enough that there's no doubt she knew what he was. She is a preter, after all. Nykk says she just lost it. She was screaming and throwing herself back, away from him, screaming that 'blood and bones' again, over and over. She didn't say anything else, just thrashed and screamed that phrase. They had to sedate her and get her to her room. She's asleep now."

"That makes it sound like vampires were involved," I commented thoughtfully. I still had nowhere near enough pieces to even have a clue, but this made a pretty strong guess that a vampire was involved in the girl's trauma. A 'happy, well-adjusted girl' didn't usually have a history of responding to a basic trigger like this so violently without someone knowing about it. I was no psychologist, but that made it pretty clear to me that it was part of the recent traumatic events.

Sam met my eyes and nodded. "Certainly makes it sound that way," she agreed. "I don't know it helps us yet, but it's important to note."

I nodded as well. There was nothing else to keep me there at that point, and the phone didn't ring again, so I headed out. I let my hand brush past hers on my way out in an attempt at inconspicuous affection. I wasn't usually prone to those kinds of things, but I was feeling a bit unsettled. It's easy to say that anyone would be after the video I'd seen, but that wasn't usually something I was prone to either. I wasn't sure why I was so affected at that moment, but

I was. It wasn't my nature to need anyone else to help me...but I did.

Still, I didn't let myself get carried away or anything.

Once I was back in my car, I just focused on work. That was always the best way past whatever ailed me. I pulled a legitimate map out of my glovebox. One of those paper ones that anyone born after 2000 probably had no idea what to do with. I started to unfold it but realized quickly that there just wasn't enough space inside my car.

As I was under a streetlight in my parking space, I was able to put it over the hood to see the whole of it. I put the map that Sam had printed for me on top and then let my eyes scan between the two. One had the useful markings but the other was bigger, giving me a better idea of the area I needed to search.

It lacked property lines, however, so that didn't help certain angles I'd want to consider. I had so little to go on, but I did know that she had been caged. Putting a preternatural in a cage was even more complicated than trapping a tiger, so I knew that some space would be needed. It also wouldn't be quiet, so there would need to be some real estate around it to not arouse the attention of the neighbors who may call the cops. I also felt fairly sure that at least one vampire was involved, so it'd need to be a place good for vamps too.

Had she been held alone or were there others? It wasn't unheard of for people to try to kidnap multiple preternatural creatures for different reasons, so I didn't want to rule out the idea that this was a wider spread matter. Then again, it might have been just about Sarita Alvarez. That made it harder, because each species needed very different space. A group would need a barn or even a warehouse, where just one victim could be held in a basement or house of some other kind.

It wouldn't be anything like apartment buildings, at least, because those would have far too many neighbors and people coming and going that made the risk of being found out skyrocket.

An isolated building of some sort, whether a house or something business sized. It wouldn't be a named business, I'd think, though, because that would make it stand out to anyone looking. Something marked on the map or listed on the internet. This had to be privately owned, even if it was a large building.

Either way, I was looking for a decently sized tract of land that could keep a building far enough away from everyone else.

I identified a couple spots that I thought seemed likely. They were big sections of forest, not near any highly populated area, and were within the search radius that the cops had given me. I folded my maps and got back in my car, heading to the first of the three I decided to hit right away.

I spent the next three hours looking over the immediate targets. I drove to each one, parked on the side of the road, and then leapt into the air. As it was, I surveyed each one with a literal "bird's eye view." It was very generalized, so I knew that I might have missed things, but I wanted somewhere to start.

Unfortunately, nothing jumped out at me—literally or figuratively—for any of the locations I surveyed. I wasn't entirely surprised, to be honest. These sorts of things always started broadly and fruitlessly, narrowing down with chance insights and pieces of evidence that would eventually lead me to the answer.

In the end, I always caught what I was after.

It was very early—or very late, depending on your perspective—by the time I got back to my house. I saw Sam's car in the driveway and felt oddly comforted to see its presence, or more that I was comforted by what its presence meant. I didn't actually have any feelings about the car itself, just the woman that drove it.

The truth was that I had never really considered myself particularly "domestic," and I had always enjoyed my alone time. I liked having my own space without anyone else in it, so I could do whatever I wanted whenever I wanted and not have to deal with any annoyances...like people.

Even so, I was secretly enjoying the way my life had turned. Maybe several decades of solitude had been enough for me? I didn't know. It was hard to say. I just knew that I would never admit it to them, but I liked having family around. It had been such a long time. I also liked having Sam around. She was the first person in a long time who I liked the presence of more than my own quiet. It might not sound like a big deal to other people, but it was a big deal to me.

Again, I wouldn't actually admit these things out loud to anyone, but I knew the truth.

I parked and headed inside, finding Sam and Buster in the kitchen. Sam wasn't really the "domestic" type either, but she was a much better cook than I was. My skills tended to be locked in the areas of re-heating, but Sam could actually, you know, cook food. Cut stuff up, mix, add seasoning and spices, and so on.

She heard the door and turned, smiling at me as I walked in. "Hey there," she said before turning back to the stove. She pulled something out of the oven and set it on the stovetop before turning to face me fully. I moved in to kiss her and then peered over her shoulder to see what she'd been making. I saw a pot of pasta and sauce. The oven seemed to have put forth a dinner bread of some kind.

"Smells good," I said.

"The very finest the supermarket shelves could offer." She smirked and turned back to the stove. Food was put in dishes and then carried out to the living room, since we weren't so high-flying in life to actually use the dining room table. That would just be *silly*.

"I imagine if you had any luck tonight, you'd have led off with that," Sam commented once we had settled in and started eating.

"Now I see why you're so good at your job," I replied with a smirk but then sighed. "And you're right. I didn't find shit on my first few tries, but this was always going to be a crapshoot to begin with. It's just too broad an area, too many possibilities."

Sam nodded. "Hence us asking for your help. We can't do any more with this ourselves, and I can't tell you how fucking frustrating that is." She shook her head with a piece of garlic bread half-raised to her mouth. "It's not like it's just our people who are seeing budget cuts, of course. I know we aren't being singled out or something, but still, one wants to feel like they can do their job."

Of course, that did make me think of something. "If the budget is so short, how are you going to pay me?" I was doing okay across the board, so it wasn't like I needed this money to make rent or something, but one didn't like being taken for granted.

"Honestly, paying you costs less than paying a whole task force salary and benefits," she pointed out. "You're not cheap, but you don't cost as much as an entire department."

"Fair," I replied, eating half my bowl of pasta before I even considered speaking again.

Dinner was very good, and it was definitely better than whatever I would have come up with if I'd been left to my own devices. Generally, work was the only thing I did well when left on my own. Buster was bumping his hard blocky head into my leg over and over, hoping that I'd give him something, but I didn't know if any of what I had was good for him, so I had to decline. I'd give him some dog treats later. It wasn't like he didn't get plenty, anyway.

"I was thinking that maybe I could take a look through the missing persons files and see if there's any Carson, figure out why she kept saying that name?" I asked with my mouth half-full of food. She didn't comment on it. She was used to me being a beast.

"Sure, I can set that up."

We both nodded and then were quiet for a few minutes.

"No developments on your end?" I finally asked,

politely waiting until my mouth wasn't full before speaking this time.

She shook her head and sighed heavily. "Alvarez has been under sedation since that call you were there for. I guess she started to come out of it at one point but just started screaming again."

I felt discomfited again, when I tried really hard to keep myself separated from such emotional reactions. "What on earth happened to her..."

"That's what we have to find out," Sam said, "yet I can't say that I truly want to know, even if I have to know...you know?"

"I know," I said, but I had to chuckle—if quietly—at the wordplay. "I can make a bunch of educated guesses, and they are all bad. I'm no psychiatrist, though—"

"And thank God for that."

"—yes, thank you."

We both half-laughed and sat in one another's company for a while as we finished our dinner. Somewhere partway through, I remembered to thank her for making food and feeding me.

After the dishes were done, I gave Buster his treats and took him for a quick jaunt outside before the three of us turned in for the night. Sam and I got settled in far more quickly than the dog, who mostly just readjusted how settled we were to make room for himself. I couldn't be annoyed, though. He was the one creature I'd ever known that was legitimately too cute for me to be mad at.

For some reason, I found it hard to fall asleep. Sam seemed to drift off pretty quickly, as I could tell from the change in her breathing and heartbeat. Buster was close behind her, but I seemed to linger awake for a while. Sleep had always been a rather hit-or-miss a thing for me, of course.

Eventually, though, sleep found me.

The year is 1625, and I'm in the throes of early adolescence. We all are, of course, since as far as any of us know or have been told, all six of us are the same age. Our parents do not really talk about it, but it gives credence to the idea that we are birthed more like litters of animals than we are like humans. Still, I somehow always felt *like the oldest.*

In the depth of puberty, even if I do not know what it is called then, I wonder about my own future. Will I ever have a family? It's hard to imagine how it will be possible, given that we don't know any others like us. We only know our own family. Can we have families with humans? None of us know. Or, really, none of us kids know. If our mother or father know, they certainly aren't telling us. Not that we'd ever actually ask. That just isn't done. It's improper and sinful for us to even be thinking of such things, but it is hard not to wonder.

All the other girls in the village, who are just a little older than I am, are already getting married. A couple are already with child. How can one not begin to wonder what a few years into the future will look like for me? I won't get married, because how can I wed a human man, but then the others in the village will wonder why I'm not getting married.

They already look at my family as if we are strange, as if we are...other. Something unknown, maybe dangerous. No one says anything of course, and they let us into the church each day, but you can just tell by the way they look at us. There is no mistaking the mistrust in their eyes. None of us speak of it, except me and Hannah sometimes. When it is dark and we are in bed, or we are far afield in the forest and are certain none of the others are around. We worry what our parents will say if they know we see it, and we don't want to scare the others if they haven't noticed.

It is bad enough that we have, we say. We wish we hadn't.

Wouldn't it be nicer to live without knowing such things? Wouldn't it be nicer to live like humans...to live normal lives and have the things that the others will have...

I woke up with a groan, completely disoriented. In my mind's eye, I saw the old forests of Germany—as it was now called, at least. I saw the haunts of my childhood, which was so long ago. Yet I knew I was not in those forests. I was in a bed. I wasn't alone in that bed, either. The other body in the bed was...

Okay, I was being slapped on the shoulder.

"My god!" Sam murmured with exasperation. "For all those poised, animalistic instincts, you sure can be a fucking rock sometimes."

"Wha— What the fuck is going on?" I groaned, peeling one eyelid open to see that she was half-buried under her pillow even as she was pushing against me.

I answered my own question a moment later when I turned my head and saw Buster's face staring very intently into mine. I knew that look. He must have whined and pawed at her when he couldn't rouse me, and she in turn did the job for him. I couldn't blame either of them, of course. He had to go, and he was my dog.

Crawling out from the warm haven of my bed beside my girlfriend, I groped around for my clothes and put them on for my best disheveled homeless person chic before slipping into sandals inappropriate for New England autumn and snagging Buster's leash to take him for his walk.

Not that he really needed a leash because he was so well-behaved, but I brought it just in case we wanted to venture further afield than our own property. He was dancing with urgent little tippy-taps by the time I opened the door, all but bolting out into the yard to take care of business. After that was done, we finished a more proper—if still short—walk before returning to the house.

As I was coming up the driveway, Edward and Lorelei joined me after the latest round of caretaking in the massive and ever-expanding kennel situation we had. It took up most of their time, but it seemed to make them happy.

"Good morning," my brother said with a smirk as he took in my appearance.

"Is it morning?" I mumbled back. I hadn't even looked at the time.

He shrugged. "Close enough." He opened the door, letting us girls and dog go first, to where Buster snagged his treat and ran off, then me and the other people on two legs went into the kitchen for our own treat—aka coffee. Sam was already there working some sort of magic on the coffeepot, and I instantly forgave her for the way she woke me up. I could sometimes be a dead lump first thing in the morning, after all. Her method of waking was still better than Buster pawing my scalp.

Once I had taken my usual seat on the counter instead of a chair like civilized people, I drank half a boiling-hot cup and winced with the pain and odd exultation of it. Then I was able to open both eyes most of the way and look around.

I noticed something off. Some folks might say I wasn't really the most observant of people when it came to emotions or 'vibes,' but that wasn't the case. I mean, cement block empath and all, but there are other ways to read things. Small patterns to be recognized, even if I didn't always say what I recognized. Being observant is actually a really important aspect of my job. As is keeping my trap shut at certain times. Now, however, wasn't one of those times.

"Are you alright?" I asked, my eyes focused on Lorelei.

Her large, dark eyes blinked at me and then she... smiled shyly? It was getting weirder by the moment. I had noticed she wasn't drinking any coffee, when she was the worst caffeine addict in the room. She was worse even than me, and that was saying a hell of a lot. She had to have been sick or something...though she didn't look sick, and the shy, almost...abashed expression seemed to say not-sick?

Edward looked at me with surprise, and Sam looked at me with confusion. She hadn't caught on to what I had, though I was sure those cop instincts would have soon. She just didn't have the direct line-of-sight that I had at that moment to notice.

I was almost regretting asking, since I didn't like the awkward feeling, yet Lorelei was one of the very few people in this world that I cared at all about. And if something happened to her, before its due course of nature, it would kill my brother...and I wouldn't let that happen.

"Yeah, I'm fine," she said with an embarrassed laugh. "I'm great, actually."

"How can anyone be great without coffee in the morning?" I blurted out in disbelief.

That made her laugh. "Okay, that part is hard, but I have to limit my caffeine for a while."

My brows knit. For all my observant nature, I did not see coming what was about to smack me full in the face.

Edward could tell that I wasn't putting the pieces together. He laughed. "She's pregnant, Anna," he said, using my childhood name to really drive the moment home.

There was an extended moment of silence before Sam did something that just made the surprise even worse... She practically *squealed*. I had never heard her make that noise before, and I had heard her make quite the noises at times. This caught me almost as off guard as Edward's news had. Sam clapped her hands and jumped up to rush in for a hug with Lorelei, who laughed again and hugged her back.

I just stared at my brother. There was something very strange and uncomfortable in the pit of my stomach. "How the fuck did that happen?"

"After four hundred years, I would think you knew the answer to that one," he replied with a smirk, but his expression softened. "I get it, and I don't know the answer. It certainly wasn't anything that we thought possible, but I guess our genetics are not quite as divergent as we thought."

"I...guess not," I mumbled, blinking rapidly and hiding my confusion behind a long drink to finish off the rest of my molten java.

Edward eyed me curiously, and I knew he was seeing more than I wanted him to, so I hopped off the counter and moved forward to hug him. We didn't do that very often, but certain occasions warranted it. This would seem to be one of them, even if I didn't necessarily feel it. He hugged me back until I let go, turning to hug my sister-in-law next and murmur "congratulations" to both of them.

The conversation dissolved into rapid, semi-coherent words mostly dominated by the girls while Edward and I—ostensibly 'the guys,' despite my biology—were relegated to coffee-drinking silence.

CHAPTER FIVE

That didn't last for much longer before Edward and Lorelei headed off, leaving Sam and I to eat breakfast-lunch. It was our first meal of the day, but it was also afternoon, so breakfast-lunch, because I wasn't posh enough to have brunch.

Having a little time to get used to my brother's bombshell news had not helped me to actually do that, unfortunately, so I wasn't 'all there' while we ate. Sam talked, and I tried to engage. I really did. When we got back together after our breakup, I swore to work on my habit of removing myself emotionally at the drop of a hat. To be fair, I had made a lot of progress, but sometimes, things were just too much.

I could tell that she noticed, but she was kind enough to not say anything. *Yet.* It would come around again, I was sure, but she was going to give me some time to process before tackling that one, and I sincerely appreciated that.

We showered and dressed for the day, heading down to the station. It was too early for Sam's shift that night, but she came with me to help look through the missing person reports to see if anyone named Carson turned up. I wasn't sure what sort of answers that might give us, but it might be something. You couldn't know what information would benefit you until you dug it up. That was my experience, at least.

Given that it was the twenty-first century and all, we were totally up to date on technological advances with the big ole stack of paper files that Sam dropped on the table in front of me.

"I confined it to people who went missing within a twenty-five-mile radius, for now, and within a couple weeks of the timeframe when Alvarez was taken," she explained as she took a seat across from me.

"It's a reasonable place to start," I agreed. Looking at the stack, I sighed heavily. "That's more than I was expecting."

She made a quiet noncommittal noise. "I mean, truth be told, a lot of these people will turn up just fine in the near future. People take off for all sorts of reasons and don't want to tell others about it for all sorts of other reasons. Not even everyone who files a report cares that much about who they're reporting, they just feel obligated."

I pursed my lips slightly as I side-eyed her. "I appreciate the rosy glow."

"If you were suited to dating a rose-colored-glasses type, you wouldn't have ended up with a cop," she pointed out.

She was right, of course. Super Idealist or Absurd Optimist types would have shriveled and died in a relationship with me. I could be a bitch, but I wasn't enough of a bitch to do that to anyone.

We got to work. Neither of us had any idea if

Carson was even a person's name, but it was a good guess. Was it a first or last name? If it was a person, I could only hope that it wasn't some weird nickname. Those sorts of details didn't always turn up in these reports, but first and last names—sometimes even middle names—usually did. We couldn't even make an educated guess about gender to narrow it down that way. Carson felt like a pretty gender-neutral first name, and obviously even more so if it was a surname.

I scanned my way through the first few files, checking all the names and then the notes, in case it was a nickname or maybe a birthplace. Someone could be from somewhere named Carson in another state but had the misfortune to vanish here.

It made for slow work, however, since one didn't want to miss something, and these forms struck me as...counterintuitive. Or I was grumpy. Or both. One could never be sure with me, really.

After about three days, which was probably closer to one or two hours, I was on my tenth file when I got a hit.

"Hey," I said, gesturing toward Sam without looking up. I could audibly tell that she was coming back to the table after getting a cup of coffee. "I think I found something."

A moment later, I felt her standing over my shoulder, leaning down to read the file along with me. I was smacked in the nose by the smell of her honey-scented shampoo and distracted for a moment before she started reading aloud.

"Carson Wilkes," she said thoughtfully. "Twenty-seven, human psychic. Cryomancer."

"He lives and works here in Adelheid," I continued, shaking off my olfactory issue. "A paralegal for Barnes, Brown, and Associates. I guess he's an associate." I kept reading. "His office reported him missing ten days ago when he didn't show up for work for two days in a row without calling. The notes say he is very conscientious."

I felt Sam nod just to the right of my head. "Cops did a wellness check at his house, but he wasn't there, so Jay Barnes filed the report."

Without looking, I reached up and took the coffee mug from her hand. She let out a little squawk of protest but didn't stop me as I took a drink and then handed it back to her. I could feel her half-hearted disapproval but didn't apologize. (Apologies were hard for me, so I reserved that much effort for when I really fucked up. Stolen sips of coffee didn't qualify in my mind.)

"Any chance we can find out if maybe there's an unnamed person recently found that they haven't been able to identify? I know it takes a while to go through these things to match them sometimes. Maybe it's been overlooked but he's turned up like Alvarez did."

"It's possible," Sam agreed, setting the mug down on the table next to me while she went to her computer. Fortunately, all the tedious paper hunting had distracted me from my unsettled feelings earlier, allowing me to smirk as I took the mug and sipped some more from it before getting up to follow her to the desk.

She was typing and tapping her way through the archaic, arcane labyrinth that composed the digital entry to law enforcement databases.

It didn't help, now that she was at her desk, that she felt compelled to answer the phone whenever it hit five rings without anyone else answering it. "They roll over," she explained as she hung up. "If no one else gets it, it comes to my desk."

"Not usually Grand Central here," I commented, giving her the coffee back.

"Not usually," she agreed. "We've had more than the usual number of missing persons reports, though, as you've seen. A lot of cars are getting stolen lately in the area as well. Some of it is rolling over from other towns that we're working with on all of it, since they are understaffed and underfunded as well."

She logged into the database and pulled up a search for unidentified males. There was a recent hit from Uncasville, where a dead body had been found but not yet identified. It was living in the "holding pattern" waiting for a full post-mortem with just the start of a file in the system. The basics in the report matched what we had on Wilkes, and his condition—minus the dead part—otherwise seemed similar to Alvarez when she'd been first found.

Sam turned to pick up the phone and call the M.E. office, but it rang instead. She answered, made it through a terse, brief conversation with someone on the other end, then hung up. She lifted the receiver again quickly to forestall another interruption and put in the call she actually wanted to.

I wasn't a part of this, so I turned back to the file. There wasn't much else in it, though. Wilkes's bosses didn't necessarily know a lot about the guy, understandably so, and couldn't put much detail into the report. No close next of kin, but some cousin in Montana would be called if the body matched.

My brain snagged on an odd detail, which wasn't really anything about Carson Wilkes but about myself... Just a few years ago, that would've been me. Hell, even less. My boss would have been the only person to notice if I never turned up again, and there wouldn't have been any family to contact. Back then, I had thought I was the only surviving member of my entire bloodline...then Hannah appeared. Unfortunately, she'd gone dark side and now was definitely gone for good. But Edward had appeared too. Then Sam. Then Lorelei...

Now, a niece or nephew?

My brain tried to fizzle out again, but I was saved by Sam turning around in her spinny computer chair. "I've got a call into the medical examiner, but I didn't get through to anyone but the receptionist. She said she'd have someone call us back when they were available, but maybe they're busy now too."

I frowned slightly. "Honestly, that is not a business that I want to be so busy."

"Agreed, but it could be any number of things. We'll just have to wait and see what they say when they actually do call me."

"Indeed," I said with a nod. My frown deepened, and I stuffed my hands in my pockets, looking around as I tried to arrange my thoughts. "Call me when you hear from them? I'm going to head out and try to check on some more things."

"No problem," she agreed. "Just be careful—"

The phone rang again. She made an exasperated expression before smiling apologetically at me, turning to answer it. I shrugged slightly and headed out.

CHAPTER SIX

Once I was back at my car, I pulled the map out again. It was still light out, so that made it easier to see the paper and the marks I had made on it. I picked a spot that I hadn't gone to yet and headed that way. I didn't really have a specific idea about that location. It was a bit of a dart-throw, all told, since there wasn't any new information to distinguish one from another.

I drove there. I could have, technically, flown everywhere, but flying was tiring. I was used to this bipedal human form or quadrupedal mammal forms, and fighting through something I had no muscle memory for took more energy than things I was more accustomed to. On my way, though, I couldn't help but spend a lot of time thinking. There wasn't much else to do while driving if you were alone in a vehicle.

Admittedly, I was still stuck on the kid thing... although I couldn't really figure out *why*, aside from shock. The more I drove, the more I thought, until I nearly drove past the turnoff I wanted. I got it just in time and with only one other car honking at me from the highway as I pulled off suddenly. I parked at the overlook and got out. I needed the other side, so I locked the car up and started to cross the two-lane roadway.

Was it really my brother becoming a father (the biological way) that bothered me? Some, yes, but only because it brought up so many questions that had been so long unanswered from our youth... That didn't seem truly upsetting, though. So, what was it?

I started crossing the road and pulled up short in a hurry when I realized I'd not noticed a car heading my way. I instantly jumped back and chastised myself for my lack of focus.

It was Sam's reaction, I decided when I was *safely* halfway across the street.

The topic of children had never come up between us, for some obvious and some not obvious reasons. As two women, it would take a far more concerted effort, but I also just assumed neither of us wanted kids. She had never shown any signs of being particularly kid-crazy, and my history with small humans was well-documented as...unfortunate. I just wasn't really... kid-friendly. Resting bitch face, cursed like a sailor, randomly made scary noises, was typically armed in some way... Yet she had just seemed so...*excited* by Lorelei's news, and that made me wonder if I'd been assuming wrong.

Once I'd made it to the other side without getting flattened, I worked to focus my absurd thoughts and look around me. I stalked into the tree line, so I was out of sight of passing cars, and then paused to inhale deeply. I closed my eyes. There was a hint of something on the wind, so I shifted to a form with a more robust olfactory sense and pressed my face to the ground.

Something preternatural. That didn't necessarily mean anything, but it was at least a *something* I could pursue, however thin it was.

Thus, that's what I did.

The trail wound through the trees, and it had some hint of confusion. It wasn't even easy to explain what I meant by that. It was just a sense of something. It wasn't a vampire, since there was no scent of the grave among it. Fae were impossible to tell from their scent. It was just too much...weird. It was clearly some kind of animal, but there were other animal scents becoming more intense the deeper I got into the forest, so it started to get a little tricky to pick out which animal sat alongside the preternatural one.

Eventually, I stumbled on something that seemed out of place in an otherwise very...*foresty* forest. It was a fence. There was a wire running along the wooden slats, which I identified as being electric. Maybe some farmer had livestock here in the woods? That was really odd, but not unheard of. I wasn't too worried about the electric fence, however, since they had such weak current that it didn't bother my supernatural strength.

So, I didn't bother to change my shape. I just slunk forward and lowered myself to slide underneath it.

That's when I got a surprise.

This was not a normal electric fence. I couldn't know what had been done to it, but the shock it gave me was so strong, it forced me out of form. I shifted back to human, flipping over on my back. My stomach brushed the line again, and I screamed "*FUCK*" as I kicked myself away from the fence as fast as inhumanly possible.

Panting, sweating, and feeling the hellish stinging on my back and stomach, I pulled up the bottom of my shirt to look at my abdomen. Even through the shirt, there was a violent, visible red line. I turned slightly wide, very horrified eyes to the fence. What the hell was *that*?!

Once I got past my surprise and the pain, I realized that this was actually a big hint that I had gotten a hit with this choice of location...

I turned back in the direction I'd been going and shifted into my mountain lion form, as it was always my first choice after human and oddly felt safer. I pressed my nose to the ground again and started moving forward. As I progressed, I started picking up more distinctly preternatural scents. Some of them were more identifiable than others. I started picking up those traces of vampires. Wolf scents became more prominent, so I knew there had been werewolves through here. There was a great variance of ages, though. Some had been here for a long time. Others were newer. It was really a big mix in the nose.

I noticed a couple of 'private property' signs nailed into trees. I did pause at that, for just a moment, thinking about my cop girlfriend. She probably wouldn't be thrilled with my trespassing since I didn't have a lot of evidence that this was the place I needed...but then, really, I didn't need the same sort of proof that cops did. I had different rules and restrictions in my job, so it would probably be fine.

That determined, I kept moving.

Up ahead was another electric fence, but I

was smarter this time. I shifted into a little bird and flittered my happy ass high enough to clear the wires without issue. I landed on the other side and shifted back. I once again became mired in the multitude of scents covering the ground. The deeper I got, the more I began to catch the tang of something that I believed to be blood. It wasn't pronounced enough to be totally sure, but it was enough to be pretty sure. I had smelled enough of it in my time, after all.

Shame on me, however, because I was so lost in trying to detect all of these wild, mixed-up scents that I wasn't fast enough to catch the one smell that belonged to someone who was...

...still here.

It was a human. I knew that in an instant. A moment later, I also recognized that it was a human with a gun. A rifle. In some kind of uniform. Some sort of guard? Some sort of unhappy guard. The gun was turning toward me.

Well, fuck.

I shrieked to throw him off guard for a moment before leaping. He got the shot off, but I was already in motion. I landed on his chest, digging in my claws just enough to stop my forward momentum then springboard right off while he was scrambling in the dirt. I took off into the trees and was well out of his sight by the time the second shot was fired.

As soon as I knew he couldn't see me, I was on wings and flapping out of the forest.

It took me a little while to get to the turnoff where I had parked my car because I'd gotten all turned around in my sudden, startled aerial departure. I had been oriented based on scents and land markers and moving on paws. The abrupt change to bird mode had me all turned around, and it took me a bit to calm my adrenaline enough to get sorted out.

Of course, there was one other thing that made it tricky.

My car was fucking gone.

I flapped around the turnoff a couple times, second-guessing my memory as to whether this was actually where I had left it. I even flew around in some high-up circles to check other areas and see if it was there, but it wasn't. I had been right the first time. My car was just bloody missing. Where the hell could it have gone?! I wasn't in the forest that long!

Just in case anyone connected to that guard was watching this area, I didn't change back into human or cougar form. Instead, I landed on the spot where my car had been on spindly little bird feet and stomped around. I was sure that would look weird if anyone was watching, but my restraint had limits. I had to do something to burn off my aggravation and let me think. Plus, I wasn't used to flying that much and had to ground myself for a while. A feathered temper tantrum sounded like just the right compromise.

It helped, a tiny bit. I didn't really feel any calmer, but a few minutes of rest was enough to let me fly again. I hovered over the road and looked in either direction, then I had a suspicion that whoever took it was heading toward town. So, I started flying along the road in that direction.

As it was particularly difficult to keep track of

time while in any animal form, and especially with so much focus having to go into just flying, I really had no sense of how much time was actually passing as I made my way along the air currents. Eventually, finally, I spotted a tow truck. My sight in this form wasn't actually as good as a normal bird of prey, which was one of the few times I didn't get all the perks when I took on an animal body. Still, it was enough. I was able to recognize the shape and color of my car. The number on the license plate confirmed that it was mine, and I dived sharply.

Naturally, I didn't plan to take on a tow truck cruising along the highway...although the thought did occur to me for a moment. Instead, I landed on the roof of my own vehicle and held on. I pressed myself low to get out of the wind flowing over the top, but the truck itself held back the worst of it.

While waiting for the truck to come to a stop and reveal the end destination for my vehicle, I tried to figure out why it had been towed in the first place. I had used a turnoff from a public roadway...hadn't I? Had it actually been private property that close to the road once I was off the road and parked? I wouldn't have thought so, but I guessed it couldn't be ruled out. My car hadn't been there long enough for anyone to think it was abandoned, though I suppose no one was around to see that and someone might have assumed.

Whatever the actual answer was, my mood was growing darker by the moment.

After another indeterminate amount of time, I peeked up and saw civilization approaching. I considered just riding the car all the way in but then figured that would be noticeable. Instead, I spread my wings and let the air carry me upward. I hovered and watched for a moment before following the truck through a couple city streets until reaching an impound lot. So annoying.

Once I confirmed that this was the lot my car was going into, I flew around to find a quiet, unpopulated place to land and shift back into my human form. I kept to my preferred body, which was 6'0" tall and leanly muscled. I had mixed up my usual hairstyle these days to still be short but a little longer on one side over my forehead, at Sam's suggestion. I felt like a sucker, but she was a pretty girl, so there you have it. Brown hair, brown eyes. I kept that.

Once I was settled into my form, with jeans, biker boots, tank top, and leather jacket, I strolled down the sidewalk and around the corner. I headed straight to the guard booth beside the tall gates and up to the window. A slack-jawed fella—who kind of looked like he'd died last week but hadn't been told—eventually slid the glass aside. Hollow eyes with big bags under them met mine, and if he thought anything about my appearing before him, he didn't say. Honestly, my Resting Bitch Face was well practiced, so the non-reaction was a little insulting. Then again, I was already in a bad mood.

"You have my car," I drawled.

He blinked slowly. "And?"

My brows lifted slightly. "Give it back."

The man had the audacity to just stare at me, and I had to resist the urge to check his pulse to see if I'd actually lost him...or smack his head into the glass until a personality came out. Whichever intrusive thought won first.

"Give me my car?"

"I can't do that."

"And...why not?"

The bastard actually shrugged, and I felt my blood pressure rise.

"If you want to keep your brains safely contained inside your skull, I would give me an actual answer and not something that a teenager could get slapped for," I said as calmly as I could manage. Truth be told, I wouldn't actually brain the guy...but I could certainly make him believe that I wanted to. Cause I did want to. I just wouldn't.

"All release orders have to come from the main office." He gave me an answer, but he was oddly unfazed by me. That was disconcerting.

I nodded, pressing my lips together to stop whatever other words were about to come out, and turned away from the booth. I walked away to save myself from an assault charge and pulled out my phone, dialing Sam's number. She answered after four rings, and I figured the office phone still had to be going a lot.

"What's up?" she asked, trying to not sound curt and harried but even I could tell that she was. I felt a little bad for not thinking this call through a little longer.

"My car got towed, and I..." What did I actually expect? "I don't know. I thought dating a cop might give me a get your car out of jail free card." I winced at myself. "I'm sorry, Sam. The guy at the booth pissed me off and I didn't think this call through. I know you're busy."

I had learned how to apologize without being prompted when I determined it was called for. See? Personal growth.

She gave me a little laugh, which at least meant she wasn't going to yell at me. I hated it when she yelled at me. "I wish it were, but unless it was towed from a public street here in Adelheid…" She trailed off, waiting for me to say if that was what happened. I admitted that it wasn't. "…then I can't do much."

"Right, right," I sighed. "Okay, I will figure it out." I blew out a breath. "Love you."

"Love you too. Good luck."

I stuffed my phone back into my pocket with far more force than was necessary and prepared myself to head back to the booth to find out what I needed to do to get paperwork through the main office and get my fucking car back…

CHAPTER SEVEN

I didn't kill anyone.

I thought I deserved a bloody gold star for my restraint but didn't think anyone was going to jump at the chance to give me one. I finally found out the process and paperwork to get my car back, but I also learned that it wasn't an instantaneous thing. Instead of walking off to find something to entertain myself with, I plunked my happy ass down on the sidewalk beside the impound lot's gate and messed around on my phone.

Admittedly, reading news articles didn't do anything to improve my mood. When did it ever? Still, I read it anyway...for a while. Then I doom-scrolled the one social media app I had on my phone until I got bored. As I was trying to figure out what to do next while waiting for the eternal hell of paperwork to get done, I had text alerts pop on my phone.

It was Sam.

The dental records match the Carson we found. Dead 3 days. Found 1 mile from where we got Alvarez. Similar signs of torture, restraint, etc., Died by blood loss. Walked some while, like Alvarez, but didn't have her preternatural stamina. Let you know when I have more. Love you.

I appreciated how long it probably took to type that out, and so cleanly, since phone keyboards were sincerely shit. No amount of technological upgrades could ever fix that fact. They seemed like they were designed to just screw with people, make you doubt your place in reality, since you could be 110% sure you were hitting the A and it would still type out Q instead.

The content of the message got to me too. So, Alvarez kept saying the name Carson in her break-with-reality fugue, and there was a dead guy named Carson who shared various signs that he had gone through things like Alvarez had... It was clearly important information, but what the fuck was actually going on?

"Hey," Walking Corpse called to me. "Car's ready."

I got my car and left as fast as inhumanly possible. Straight back to the house and through the window to avoid having to talk to anyone. Buster didn't even bark because he could smell me through the glass. I gave him one of the treats I kept in my nightstand, and he settled in to eat it while I pulled my laptop from the shelf.

Part of me considered calling Sam to help dig up some more information, but I thought better of it. I was feeling pretty grumpy anyway, so maybe it was nicer to not bother my girlfriend about stuff. Probably abusing the privilege or something. It was my own job too, so best that I do it.

Opening a browser, I spent a few minutes trying

to recall the address of where I'd been. I got close enough, I figured, to look stuff up. It took some time on map apps and squiggling with my cursor, but I finally hit on what I wanted.

It looked like the area I'd been in was listed as some kind of "nature preserve," even though it was owned by a corporation. Then again, what wasn't these days? I could get the name of the business, at least: Lucas Enterprises. That was founded by Gino Lucas, who was the current CEO. The business was based out of New London, although the language about what Lucas Enterprises actually did was a lot of…corporate-speak that ultimately explained almost nothing. I read a few pages of their website and came away not at all wiser. All I got was some kind of "research and development." Also that the business started in 2006, before Cameron's Law, but it had worked to adapt and expand since.

Next, I tried to look up Gino Lucas, but everything about him seemed like a stereotypical hermit rich guy. There were only a couple pictures available and honestly, they looked like something from a stock photo site. Few public sources otherwise. I wondered if maybe he was a preternatural himself, but I couldn't find anything about that. It could be good PR to be open about that these days so it would be surprising to still hide it. Some folks did, though, so it wasn't impossible. Still, it was weird to find so little about the guy. It seemed there was no family of note—no spouse or children.

I looked at the time. Nothing suggested this Lucas or his HQ kept preter hours, so I figured I'd go scope him out tomorrow morning…

The rest of my night was pretty boring. I texted with Sam a few times, doing my best to not be bitchy since she didn't deserve that, but she was really busy at the station so it was only a few short messages. Eventually, Buster and I just went to sleep. In the morning, it was the usual symphony of barking dogs. I took my own for his walk, and then I set out for New London.

I didn't want to park right outside the guy's business, just in case someone would get particular and take a look. I did not need my car impounded for a second time, after all, so I tried to play it careful and parked at a diner. I sat in my car for a little bit, trying to decide how I wanted to go about this. Since I could make my face and body look pretty much any way I wanted, there were a lot of options. The real decision to be made was about the story I wanted to tell.

For the hell of it, I decided to make a scene.

I looked around to see if anyone was looking at my car. When the coast seemed to be clear, I shifted my physical form. It wasn't like a big secret that I was a shapeshifter anymore, but it still creeped people out. It also would give up my game if people saw the face I started with and the one I ended up with.

Today, I chose to go from my usual 6' "butch" self to a petite, very pregnant blonde. Obviously, it was just an affect in the shape of my midsection, as even my strong shifting skills could not create a baby, but…

The shape I chose was good to make a splash, but after a moment's consideration, it caused something weird to twinge in my chest. It made me think about all those things that I didn't want to think, so I did what I usually did when that happened: ignored it, stuffed it down, and just got grumpy. I mean, a therapist would undoubtedly say that wasn't the right way to do it, but it had been my way for several hundred years...

Getting out of my car, emotions appropriately stuffed and subverted, I walked down the sidewalk and around the corner. I tried to approximate the right walk for the condition I was pretending to be in, and I just hoped no one looked that close. I walked straight through the large, glass double-doors with "Lucas Enterprises" over them, heading for the huge, semi-circular reception desk. I couldn't help but notice it was marble, clearly expensive. My brain, having always been frugal till I dropped my life savings on my current property and dog rescue, couldn't fathom why someone would need this kind of desk to answer phones at...

That was beside the point.

"I need to see Mr. Lucas," I declared to the woman sitting behind the mausoleum of a desk. I tried to affect my best Midwestern accent alongside a suitably distressed expression, although neither had ever been my strong suit.

"I'm sorry, but Mr. Lucas is not available right now," the woman replied without a single bit of hesitation or even taking a moment to check a schedule. She had *Rich Bitch* all over her expression, posture, makeup, hairstyle, clothing, and diction...but when I looked a little closer, I got the feeling that it was its own affectation. She probably wasn't born to it, which meant overcompensating. That made her unlikely to be sympathetic to me, but I was committed to the bit now.

"Please," I simpered. "He'll want to talk to me. Leslie? Leslie Burton? He knows me... He knows me..." I looked downcast for a moment, letting my eyes drop to my stomach. "...*very* well. And I really need to speak with him."

She arched one overly plucked eyebrow and looked me up and down like I was a cockroach she'd just found in her cabinet. I waited for a high heel to land on me at any moment. I couldn't see her shoes from here, but I had a good guess. "Look, I don't know who you are or what you want, but I know that you have no valid reason to speak with Mr. Lucas. Please leave."

I made my eyes get big, like I was going to cry. I couldn't actually create tears on command, that was a bit much for my abilities as a shifter or actor, but I could look like I was about to. "What do you mean? That's... I... I have every reason to see Gino! Please, let me just speak to him for a moment. I promise, I won't be any trouble—"

"Guard!" the receptionist called, lifting herself from her seat slightly to look just down the way to where a secret-service-looking guy was standing. He turned at her call. "This woman is some sort of imposter. Please escort her out of the building. If she resists, call the cops."

Well, that escalated quickly.

He moved toward me, and I spun fast on my heel to make a quick retreat. There was something unnerving about how certain she was that I was a fake. Rich men being rich men, how unusual would it be for a pregnant woman to show up...

I really didn't feel like letting this bozo get his hands on me, however, so I just got out of there before he could. I was annoyed that my ruse was seen through that fast and I couldn't even get an attempt at a foot in the door, so I was worried I might smack this guy and get myself in deep trouble. Out the door and around the corner faster than a pregnant woman could probably manage, but I ducked into a doorway and shifted fast back to my usual form so the guy wouldn't recognize me as the woman he just chased out. I sat on the step there, looking casual as I pulled out my phone and stared at nothing, waiting.

Sure enough, the guard came around the corner just a heartbeat later. He obviously hadn't wanted to look like he was chasing someone down on a public street, hence the few moments I had before he got there. I kept my head down, eyes seemingly glued to my phone like most folks were while I watched him out of my peripherals. He paused, looking each way down the street and then across to the other side. Obviously, he didn't spot his little, blonde pregnant lady who'd come to try to make trouble for his boss.

All of this because of a woman showing up at reception? Okay, yes, I was aiming for a scene, but this wasn't the goal. I had been aiming for an anxious exec coming downstairs to shut me up so I could get a feeling for this guy who owned the space where our victim (or victims) may have been held...and where I almost got shot. I did tend to take that a little personal and all.

The guard kept looking for a few moments before he gave up and went back around the corner, presumably back into the Lucas building.

I had a very weird feeling about this place, so I decided to stick around. Slipping my phone back in my pocket, I took a look, waited till the coast was clear, and then shifted into a seagull. Much like pigeons are everywhere in New York City, Connecticut parking lots have an odd profusion of seagulls. So, in that particularly obnoxious form, I did a little aerial surveillance. I found the entrance (and exit) to a parking garage that was under the Lucas Enterprises building. Obviously, that belonged to them. Since I spotted no other entry, I figured this was the place to watch.

So, I landed in a nice, obscure spot. Again waited for a clear coast, then shifted into a squirrel. I risked my life to cross the street to something more out in the open and positioned myself at the base of a tree for the kind of stakeout that 'regular' cops never had the pleasure of experiencing.

CHAPTER EIGHT

By the time night fell, I'd had enough time to decide that my job sucked.

I had watched every single face walking out of the front doors, although the angle was tough from my tree, and I had looked through the windshield of every car driving out of that underground parking lot. I'd been chased halfway up the tree twice by passing dogs, including one very intimidating chihuahua—they are terrifying when you're the size of a squirrel—and had one little shit of a toddler throw pebbles at me while his mother studied the bottom of her pumpkin spice latte.

When it became clear that the building was shut down for the night with only a security guard manning reception, I squeaked and hopped my way back across the street and ran into the parking garage. It was empty.

Not a single face I had seen looked like any picture of Gino Lucas I had seen online. In fact, there were far fewer people leaving altogether than I would have expected for a building this big. Was it somehow everyone's day off? That seemed weird. What also seemed weird was the receptionist not just fobbing off my pregnant lady act by saying Lucas wasn't there if he wasn't, in fact, there. She didn't have to take an attitude and sic the guard on me if she could just say he was out and I should come back some other time.

Something wasn't right about this. I could feel it. I just couldn't see exactly what it was that was off. I wasn't a psychic, but after a life like I'd lived for the past four hundred years, I had a pretty well-developed instinct. Especially for when fuckery was afoot, and I was sure that some kind of fuckery was afoot here.

I made my way back out of the garage and hurried off down the street toward the diner where I parked my car. I ran around behind it and shifted into my human form, immediately groaning. I was seated as I shifted, close to the ground, and leaned back against my tire. That was way too long to have been in that particular animal's form. The little hunched-over critters were hell on the spine.

Getting to my feet, I stretched myself out and reached high overhead. I heard at least six vertebrae crack, and I cursed.

"Rough day?" a voice asked from just off to my left.

I hadn't heard or smelled anyone approach, but then again, I was in the lot of a busy diner. Still, while I didn't show it, I was unnerved. I turned my head to see a pretty young woman, maybe a teenager, with a plastic bag full of takeout containers. She flashed a smile, which I thought was a little too innocent...but, no, I was just grumpy she snuck up on me. I usually wasn't that sloppy.

"Yeah, long day at work," I replied flatly, turning

away and heading for my driver's side door. She watched me, looking a little perplexed but not too offended. I got behind the wheel and locked my doors, but since I didn't feel like making a show of escaping a teenager, I took my phone out of my pocket.

I had several text messages, which I realized I hadn't been able to hear because, y'know, squirrel. I replied to a few, assuring the only ones I gave a damn about that I was okay. No one was too worried yet, since I often went quiet for several hours while I was working. That was just part of the job, and those who mattered would understand that. I did make sure that someone was keeping an eye on Buster, of course, but I knew that Edward and Lorelei always would.

When I looked up from my text messaging, I saw that the other woman was gone. I took a quick glance around, but I didn't see anyone.

I rolled my shoulders a few times, trying to think through what I wanted to do next. I still felt like my job sucked, but it was my job and I would do it. I took my profession seriously, even when it was boring or miserable. Today, it had been both.

There was obviously something about that piece of land. It wasn't a nature preserve, at least not the kind it was purporting to be. I didn't know if I really wanted to know what kind of "nature" was being preserved there, but things were adding up too oddly to overlook it. A plot of land with preternatural-proof-level electric fences and guards with guns who shot with very little provocation? Cars towed just for being parked in proximity? Owned by a super mysterious company that was also seemingly paranoid?

I decided to go back to the "nature preserve."

This time, I sure as hell wasn't going to park my car too close. I found a public lot this time, one of those commuter lots, and took to the sky. I flew toward the preserve and tried to get a view from high above, less chance of getting shot at, but the treetops were thick for all of my flight. It was autumn, but the leaves hadn't all fallen away, and there were a lot of evergreens to fill in the gaps there were.

At one point, however, after maybe twenty minutes of flying that my little avian back did not like after all that time as a squirrel, I spotted a building. I figured that was the best I was going to get, so I crossed my non-existent fingers, said a prayer, and flew down. The moon was bright that night, and that helped me in what I needed to do. It even broke through the treetops better than my eyesight had.

I landed in a tree that looked the safest for my shift and then, reluctantly, changed back to the rotten little squirrel. They were just such ubiquitous creatures that they lived under the radar to everything but chihuahuas. From my tree branch, I scouted the ground level but didn't see any angry dogs or guards with guns, so I skittered down the tree trunk and into the brown grass and leaf litter. I hopped along, pausing every now and then to act more like an actual squirrel, but I kept my general trajectory toward where that building had been.

Shortly, I was able to spy a building through the trees, and I squeaked my way along to it. However, I wasn't able to get too close before I heard the snorting and snuffling of dogs. Before they could get their teeth on my fluffy-tailed ass, I lunged for the nearest tree and raced upward. It was just one dog, I realized a moment later, but it was clearly well-trained because it didn't pursue me. This was a guard dog. A Malinois, if I had to guess, though I'd been more used to the pit and staffy variety these days.

I waited till the dog ran his circuit and walked away, then hopped a few branches to try to get closer to the building. I got pretty close this way and settled down on the limb to watch for a little while.

It wasn't long before a car pulled up. My fuzzy brows rose as I watched the car park, and a man in camouflage hunting gear climbed out. Floodlights aligned at the top of the building showed him clearly. It was too far, and my nose too small, to get a smell from where I sat. He was wearing sunglasses, but his face otherwise was unremarkable and unfamiliar. He stood beside the car, like he was waiting, and just a moment later, it was clear what—or who—he was waiting for.

There was a small building beside the big one that I'd spotted from the air, and from this building walked a woman. She was average height and slender build, dark complexion, carrying herself with a lot of confidence. It veritably oozed from her every pore, contained within a professional but practical pair of khaki slacks, button-down blouse, leather gloves, and a patterned headscarf.

She approached the man, and they greeted one another with a firm nod and handshake, talking about something I couldn't hear from here. My lip-reading skills weren't ideal, so that wasn't much help either. They talked for a little while as I watched, trying to pick up some clue about what was going on. It had the definite feel of...business being conducted, but in the middle of the woods? An alleged nature preserve? With a dude in camo? Hunting in the middle of the night?

Abruptly, the woman held up her hand to silence him. Her head tilted like a falcon, then she turned it...

...in my direction.

In that instant, I felt absolutely sure she wasn't just looking *toward* me but was actually looking *at* me. It wasn't paranoia. I was sure of it.

I was *really* sure of it when she pointed at me and called out. From seemingly nowhere, several guards and a couple Malinois leapt in my direction. My heart all but seized where it sat, but my survival instinct took over. I shifted into a small bird and took off straight into the sky. I heard what might have been a couple of gunshots, but I wasn't sure. No bullets came near me, so maybe they hadn't shot at me. I knew it was technically private property, so maybe they had the right to shoot at encroaching vermin, but still, I was shaken.

How had that woman known that I was something other than a squirrel? She had known, though...

She had known.

I had no idea how I made it home, but I did. My car was still in the commuter lot, I knew that much. I'd have to go get it, but that was for...later. Today, I flew all the way back to the house and practically collapsed when I reached my front door.

Every preternatural species has remarkable powers of healing, except when silver is involved.

We are resistant to almost all diseases, too. The thing most people don't realize, however, is that we can still get tired. It doesn't happen as fast as it does for humans, but it happens. We can still have adrenaline dumps that then drop us like stones when they run out, and that happened to me.

No one was in the kitchen when I unlocked the door and staggered inside. I got to my bedroom and found Buster flopped over on his back, snoring. He knew it was me before I opened the door, so he just snorted when I walked in. He smelled my distress a moment later, I was sure, because he rolled over and stared at me until I lay down beside him. We curled up together, and I buried my face against the top of his head. Something about the soft, warm fur there and the scent of his face eased my stress.

I fell asleep...or maybe I just passed out.

I am fourteen years old. I am running through the woods of Germany, but not as a human, of course. Young human women do not run alone in the forest if they're smart, but I am more than any mere human. While I may sometimes be sad for what I miss being inhuman, there are things granted to me that I cherish.

What other girl in this tiny village knows what it feels like to run through the trees as a wolf? To be free. Unfettered by the rules and constrictions of the human world...

There is one rule, however, put down by my family: no human must ever see us shapeshift.

I didn't know that there were humans hunting in the woods. I didn't know that my body could revert instinctively to a human form when I was shocked or hurt. I didn't know they could see me...

I woke up feeling like shit. Dreams of my childhood often did that to me, but with different types of lousy. This time, it was the feeling of shame. For decades, I believed it had been my fault that my family was denounced as witches...

I believed I was to blame for my father and half my siblings being burned at the stake, and for my mother shifting in front of humans to defend us and give me and one brother and one sister time to escape. And even though I learned (centuries later) that it hadn't actually been my fault, that was a burden I had carried for a long time. Even the truth could not fully shed me of it.

Trying to shake off all of the feelings, I dragged my sorry ass out of the bed and all but slid my way into the kitchen. There was already coffee made by Lorelei and Edward this morning. It was lukewarm by then, but I drank it all straight from the pot and then set it up to produce more. I went to the fridge and stood staring inside, cursing that I seemed to not have any food. Just ingredients.

When the door opened behind me, the food still hadn't magically materialized into a meal. I didn't bother getting worried about the person who came into my house because I recognized her scent in an instant. I heard the door click shut, and a moment later, Sam hugged me from behind and rested her chin on my shoulder.

Her presence brought me comfort on some

level, but unfortunately, that level was a little further inside than was ideal for the moment. Externally, I couldn't seem to respond. Like I was somehow frozen on the outside. I grunted something by way of a hello and felt her chin shift against my shoulder, giving me the image that she was pursing her lips. She made a sound that came across as noncommittal but that I'd come to recognize as a sort of generalized question.

"Bad dreams," I replied.

"It's been a while since you had dreams that make you this surly."

Sometimes, it struck me as weird that I'd now been in a relationship long enough for someone to be able to recognize that. I didn't really have the reputation of being someone that got that close to other beings.

I grabbed the first thing that looked tolerable to eat out of the fridge, and she and I moved to the couch. We both stared at our phones for a while, though I could feel her frequent looks in my direction. I never acknowledged them, even though I wanted to. I did want to tell her more about what was going on inside my head, but I just...couldn't. Like locks on doors that I couldn't undo.

Eventually, she put that together too. She kissed my cheek, said something like "I can see you need some space," and then headed out with a sigh.

I felt guilty as hell, but I just couldn't do anything about it.

CHAPTER NINE

Feeling disconcerted after what should have been a nice morning with my girlfriend, I decided to go for a run. Of course, I couldn't do this without Buster coming with me, but that was fine. He was pretty much always good company, and he'd even managed to get used to my different animal forms. That was no small feat when most the forms I took were large predators. His doggy instincts had to be screaming that I was a threat, but maybe enough of my 'me' smell remained to ease that internal conflict for him. He could run alongside my mountain lion form without any sign of it being a problem.

We ran into the forest on our property. I knew it turned into someone else's property at some point, but it had never really been an issue. I preferred being more out of sight of others, both for myself and my dog. There was plenty of forest in Adelheid, so I could pretty much always find this sort of solitude...except in my own house, but that was an entirely different matter. One that I had to keep reminding myself was entirely a problem of my own making, but that logic had never been the sort I liked so I tried to not think about it. That was easy to do when I was running full bore through the trees.

Pitbulls being incredibly athletic animals, Buster had no trouble keeping up with me despite how much larger I was in this shape. His mouth was open half the time, tongue lolling out happily as we raced toward nothing in particular. We both just needed the physical exertion. It might help keep me sane, and from being a total bitch to everyone, and it might keep him from eating the furniture when I wasn't home. So, it had the potential of being a win-win, but few could actually predict the future. Even those human psychics with the rare seer ability would still tell you that for anything beyond the very immediate future, it was always fluid. It could be changed.

Anyways, that didn't really matter now.

All that mattered in that moment was the scent of the woods and the sound of paws slamming into dirt and undergrowth. We leapt over the giant roots that stuck out of the ground and splashed directly through the small brook babbling on its way by. We dodged slippery rocks, and water splashed up from both of our steps into each other's faces. Buster couldn't actually laugh, but I imagined him doing so anyway. A doggy laugh in his doggy head...which was a phrase I'd keep to myself with happiness and never, ever let someone outside my head hear me speak aloud.

Eventually, though, I knew we needed to head home.

Buster would be tired and need food and water, and I still had a job to do.

We headed east until we reached the trees

where they lined the road that my house was on. Here, I shifted back to my human form and was pulling the leash out of my pocket—as we were on the road now—when a blue SUV came into sight, turning the corner onto my street.

It really shouldn't have caught my attention, since an SUV was common enough around here and vehicles were allowed to drive down this road, even if I might not like it...but something caught my attention anyway. Maybe half a memory, or the slow speed it moved at? I knew the speed limit here, and I knew that everyone in New England thought those were just guidelines anyway, so why was this one driving so slow? I tried to tell myself that they were just looking for a house or were lost, but I clicked my tongue against my teeth to get Buster's attention and start backing into the woods again...

He had already sensed my tension, and while he obeyed my command, his body was rigid as his eyes followed my line of sight.

Before we got back into the trees, the van sped forward and screeched to a halt right in front of us. With speed that shouldn't have been possible, the side door was open and four people in dark clothes and face masks were leaping out at me.

I wasn't one to be caught by surprise for longer than a heartbeat, and I caught the first man by the throat. He was a little shorter than I but built with similar musculature. Human, though. This one, at least. I grabbed him so quickly that his lower half kept moving forward for a moment while his top half was immobilized, like in a cartoon. He instantly started making hacking noises behind his mask when I pulled his face close to mine.

"Bad fucking choice, buddy," I hissed before forcibly thrusting him into the dirt. I heard the air wheeze out of his lungs upon impact, but I was already moving on.

Buster's snarling filled the air around us, and I heard a shriek. I couldn't really look, but I thought I saw someone trying to rip their arm free of his teeth.

Good luck with that, I thought darkly as I lunged to the right, avoiding what looked like a cattle prod coming my way. I wished I could have time to wonder who the fuck these people were and just what in the hell they thought they were doing, where they found the audacity to try this, but it all moved too fast. I dodged the zappy stick on one side but had to throw myself back from another. These two were some sort of shapeshifters, which put us on much more even footing than a human against me. It was obvious, however, that this wasn't an attempted assassination. It was an attempted kidnapping.

Idiots.

Lunging back as I had, however, had put me a little off balance. I would have preferred an upward shift but instead shrunk to a vermin and ran through the legs of one attacker. I stopped while still underneath him and shifted back to my six-foot human form to shoulder-check his crotch and throw him off my back. He landed on the first guy, who was still gasping and gagging for breath.

The other one caught me on the way up, however, and I felt a surge of electricity slam through me. It wasn't like that fence, though, so it didn't incapacitate me, but it hurt like a bitch. I screamed a half-coherent curse and spun around with my elbow leading the way. I caught some body part but couldn't see what it was because my eyes were half-closed. Maybe it was the pain, maybe the electric shock controlling some synapses, or maybe both, but it sucked. It hindered me. I didn't like flailing blindly in a flight, even just for a moment.

Still, I knew the hard point of my elbow hit something painful. I let my momentum spin me around, lashing out with my other hand and partly shifted claws. Another score. This time, I could smell the blood. A moment later, my eyes opened. I could see three people on the ground, and I turned to see where the fourth was.

In that instant, I registered that the final kidnapper had gotten loose of Buster, who had retreated a few steps and looked like he was favoring one paw. That didn't stop the tide of aggressive growling, of course.

I also registered that the last person apparently determined I was too much trouble…

…and was pointing a gun in my face.

I froze. I was good, but even I couldn't dodge a bullet. And a point-blank shot to the head may be enough to kill me.

My heart skipped a beat, and I stopped breathing. I rapidly evaluated my choices as the man, cradling one mangled arm to his chest while the other held the pistol, stared at me.

The choice was taken from me a moment later by a flying blur of brown-and-white fur. Buster had catapulted himself through the space between us, latching onto the gun-wielding arm and driving it away from me. The gun discharged half a breath later, and I could hear how close the bullet was as it whirred past my head and raced harmlessly into the forest.

The man screamed as he landed hard on the dirt, right where it met pavement, and tried to kick my dog. I was on him in an instant, punching him so hard in the face that something audibly cracked. I didn't care what. Maybe he was dead. I didn't care. Instead, I spun to see Buster leaning and whimpering.

I did something in that moment that I hadn't done in some while...

I panicked.

Grabbing Buster's dense body up in my arms, I sprinted down the street to my house. I left four bodies behind, injured or worse, without a thought to answers or arrests. They'd probably escape, but I didn't care. I had to get us home.

Even in my human form, I'm faster than the average human and strong enough to do it with a sixty-pound weight in my arms. I got back to the house in record time and all but kicked the door in.

"Edward! Lorelei!" I shouted with all the volume my preternatural vocal cords allowed.

I set him on the couch and checked him over, but I didn't see any obvious physical injuries. I was hardly a vet, though, so that did not reassure me.

My brother and his wife raced into the house a couple minutes later, my shouts causing panic in them as well since that was not something I ever did. I explained what had happened in rapid cadence and probably poor clarity, but they got the idea. Edward grabbed me by the arms to get me to look at him while Lorelei dropped to her knees beside the couch to check over my pup. She wasn't a vet either, but she had a lot of training and experience with dogs in all sorts of health and condition.

"You're okay," he said, his eyes holding mine to convey steadiness. "Buster will be okay, too. If we need to get the vet, we will. He will be cared for."

I forced myself to take a slow, deep breath and nod once.

He returned the nod and then stepped away, pulling his phone from his pocket. I didn't ask who he was calling and instead knelt beside Lorelei at the couch where Buster licked her hands as she tested his limb. She offered me a small, reassuring smile.

"I think it's just a sprained paw," she said. "We will keep a close eye on him and call in our vet if he shows anything concerning."

I swallowed hard, scratching behind his ears as he leaned his thick skull into my hand. "He saved my life. I nearly got shot in the face."

It was clear on her face that my story scared her, but she was holding steady for my sake. Or for Buster, which was totally fine. I'd much rather she fuss over him than me.

"I tried calling Sam, but it went to voicemail," Edward said as he joined us again.

"I'll go down to the station myself in a few," I said, slightly hoarse.

Inwardly, I was trying to not to overanalyze everything that had just happened and everything I was feeling. I was never really a fan of self-reflection and psychoanalysis. I tried to think I could just take everything as it was and as it happened, despite plenty of evidence from my past proving that wrong over and over. I consciously chose to not learn from those particular past mistakes.

"I think you're more worried about that dog than you would be if I was the one who had gotten hurt," he teased.

"Probably," I replied easily, even though we both knew that wasn't true.

When Lorelei had gotten hurt a while back, I'd nearly come apart at the seams and taken down a few buildings with me. But still, it was different with Buster. He was a dog, and I had more kinship with animals, and he'd gotten hurt as part of my fight. He had been protecting me.

"So, you are sure he's okay?" I asked her.

"As sure as I can be at this moment," she said.

I nodded. "Alright, I'll go down to the station to make my report." I stood, but I wasn't moving too quickly. I didn't want to leave him, but I knew that I had to tell the cops—tell Sam—what had happened, even though I still hadn't fully processed it myself yet. After looking down at him for another minute, I forced myself to turn and head for the door.

A moment later, I heard the familiar telltale thump and nail click of him jumping off the couch. His gait was uneven, and I turned to see Lorelei holding him back from following me.

"Well..." I crossed the minimal distance and bent over to pick him up. "I guess he's coming with me."

I carried Buster to my car, but by the time we reached the station, he wasn't having that anymore. Pitbulls could ride that line between wanting to be spoiled and needing to be independent quite well. He still limped slightly, but he seemed okay otherwise as we walked into the police station. He was on his leash, of course, but the uniformed officer at the front desk still didn't look enthused. She also didn't look like she recognized me.

"Ma'am…" She definitely didn't know me. "I'm sorry, but the dog has to stay outside."

"No," I replied simply, not even making eye contact as I looked over her head to peer into the squad room beyond. "Is Detective Moore here?"

"No, she's not," the uniform replied peevishly, "and you really have to leave the dog outside."

Now, I looked at her, and she blanched slightly. "I'll wait outside with him then," I said flatly. "Tell whatever officer is taking assault and attempted abduction reports that Dakota is waiting outside. They should know my name back there." I didn't wait for her reply before I was out the door with my dog.

I did wonder where my girlfriend was, since I thought she was heading in to work, but apparently not. Sadly, it was daylight, so no Vance either.

Before long, a lanky human in a uniform came out to meet me. I didn't know him by name, but I'd seen him around. He greeted me politely, even gave Buster some gentle head-pats, then sat on the bench outside with me to write out the report on a clipboard. I felt a very tiny bit bad to make him do it, but I was a little glad that my reputation earned me some latitude as well. He assured me that someone would go check out where it happened, and I let him swab a bit of blood remaining on Buster's mouth. He stuffed the Q-tip in an evidence bag and returned inside. Not exactly the usual protocol, but I appreciated it.

After that, I went to Sam's apartment, but her car wasn't there and no one answered the door. Buster and I loitered for a while, to see if she'd show, but then I figured we couldn't wait there forever. I took us to the office next, where Madison was getting set up for the night.

I explained what happened, and she agreed to dog-sit Buster for a little while. I didn't want him to be alone, and this was closer to the station than going home was. This time, I need him to stay put. I was on the hunt for some familiar faces.

CHAPTER TEN

I let myself take a little extra time before getting back to the station. This was for a few reasons.

First off, I needed to center myself again. I wasn't used to panic, which had me feeling untethered. People try to kill me kinda often, as it turns out—I work in a rough business—so that part fazed me less. I wasn't necessarily used to people *protecting* me, and something about it being this loyal pup... I don't know. It hit me really hard, and I ran around the park in town for a while to burn it off. This was a very popular area at any hour of the day or night, so I wasn't worried about being caught out again when I was here. And I needed something to get rid of the excess energy.

Secondly, after all that, I needed food. I hadn't eaten much that day and had expended a lot of energy both physically and emotionally.

And finally, I wanted it to be after dark, so the chances of catching Sam and Vance were better.

I ate a couple of rare burgers at Molly's Diner to take care of the second point. I ate there often enough that they knew how I liked things and made sure the rare was very rare. I wasn't super keen on living off things I had to kill myself, which I had done for decades once upon a time, but the animal within still needed to be sated. The staff here was used to the preternatural crowd too, so it felt pretty okay to be there.

By the time I was done, night had fallen. Autumn helped that, since dark came earlier than in summertime.

After paying my bill, I headed back to the police station. I saw Sam's car in the parking lot this time, so that was good. Better, the uniform manning reception recognized me and waved me in. I nodded once at them in acknowledgement and then went straight into the main office space. I knew my way easily to the major crimes desk and found my girlfriend and my friend/boss's husband. They were both on the phone, and they both wore aggravated expressions. Vance saw me first and nodded, holding up his hand in a 'just one moment' gesture before swatting Sam on the arm and pointing. She glanced back at me. She smiled, though it seemed a little...distant. I supposed I couldn't blame her, but it still sucked.

I found a place to wait until they were free and then approached the desk.

Now that I was there, though, I fumbled a bit. "So, ah," I began, rubbing the back of my neck. "I had an...interesting morning." From there, I delivered my best clinical explanation of what happened, but it was impossible to soften the event. I watched the concerned and surprised reaction happen in both of their faces, although obviously a little more on Sam's.

"Are you okay?" she asked with no distance remaining. She got up and put her hand on my arm, and I managed a faint smile.

"Yeah, I'm fine."

"And Buster?"

I nodded slightly. "Yeah, he's okay. Lorelei thinks he may have sprained his paw but is okay otherwise. He is hanging out at the office with Madison while I'm here."

With that out of the way, we settled back into the crime part of things.

"Since it happened, I've been thinking about that girl, the crazy one who'd been kidnapped. She talked about a blue van, yeah? This was a blue SUV. They were clearly not interested in killing me, at first."

"Until you became too much of a pain in the ass," Vance said with a wry, teasing half-smile.

I mirrored the expression. "Exactly. I'm sure you both understand the feeling."

Vance snorted. Sam rolled her eyes at our gallows' humor. She didn't find my near-death experience amusing. I supposed that wasn't a surprise.

"There's something else," I went on. Sam's brows shot up, and I tried to ignore the look she gave me by directing my revelation at Vance. I explained about the location I'd investigated where I met the guard with the gun.

"And you didn't tell me—us—about this why, exactly?" Sam drawled.

I forced myself to look at her. If I could look a gun in the barrel without flinching, I could not let myself be intimidated by this lithe 5'8" creature...who pretty much owned me. "I don't have a good excuse." I sighed, knowing I had many sins to atone for with my girl. "I wanted to check it out more to assure it was a solid lead."

The look in those pretty gray-green eyes assured me that she knew this too.

"Where was this, exactly?" Vance jumped in to ask. Being a married fella, he knew precisely when to stage an intervention.

I asked them to pull up a map on their computer and showed them. They took a few notes and then nodded to each other.

"We'll go check it out," Vance said.

Sam pointed a finger in my face. "You stay put. You've gotten yourself into enough trouble today."

"Hey! It's hardly my fault that I was nearly abducted and shot."

"Second point," she snapped, although the tone of her voice shifted a little, "we need to keep your ass safe."

I growl-grumbled but didn't argue, even though I wanted to. I had a better plan anyway. Or at least one that didn't require arguing with Sam right then.

Sam knew me well enough to at least make a good attempt at making me following her orders by waiting to leave until she'd seen me drive off.

I drove back to the office and checked on Buster, who was in a snack coma under Madison's desk. He didn't even bother to stop snoring and roll off his back when I came in, so I left him as he was and returned to my car. I drove off toward the preserve, although I stopped to park on the side of the road far short of the actual location. I didn't want them to find me. I knew I risked being towed again, but that was the better option of the two.

Taking to the sky, I flew back to the preserve and found a nice branch to hang out on. I wanted to see what happened, but I'd at least try to stay out of it. With luck, Sam would never know I'd been there.

My two favorite detectives arrived just moments after I landed. I watched as a guard came out and talked to them. They were just far enough away that I couldn't quite pick out their low-pitched conversation, but it didn't look like it was particularly fraught. The guard seemed...casual, friendly, as they spoke. Vance gestured in a way that clearly said they wanted to look around. I saw the first sign of tension then as the guard gestured the 'just one moment' sign and stepped away to speak into a walkie on his shoulder. Rather well-organized, this place.

On an impulse, I decided to check out the other side of the building. I hopped and flitted along branches until I got there, and just as I did, I spotted a woman hurrying out the back door. It only took me a moment to recognize her as the one from before, who'd spotted me in the trees. She was clearly making a run for it, concealing it by not using a car. She hurried into the forest instead, so of course I followed her.

There was clearly fuckery most foul afoot. Or... most fowl, given the form I was wearing.

I swooped down and veered between a couple of trees, keeping the woman in sight. It wouldn't be hard to keep up with a human woman running on—

That's when the woman shifted.

She went from human to a deer in an instant. In a very familiar instant. It caught me so off guard that I nearly fell like a brick, but I caught myself at the last minute.

What the fuck?!

The base-level thought got through: this bitch was a theriomorph. This bitch was like me...but that's as far as it could process in that moment.

Even if I hadn't suspected her of nefarious deeds and trying to flee the cops, there was no way I could let her get away now. I had to talk to her. As far as I knew, the only living theriomorphs were my brother and I...

How had I not smelled what she was?!

I flapped my little brown wings and put on some speed as she pranced through the trees, not quite hell bent for lecture but more than a stroll. A few moments later, I was dive-bombing her back and landed on her with the full force of a mountain lion. A strange bleating sound escaped her, and a human face hit the dirt. I was human a moment later, flipping her over.

"Who the hell are you?!" I growled, pinning her shoulders.

Her eyes, so dark as to be nearly black, widened as she stared up at me...for just a moment. She shifted an instant later into a small enough creature to wiggle out from under me and drop me to the ground. I lunged after her and caught a fluffy tail, pulling her back. The rabbit spun in my grip, flowing smoothly into a coyote that snapped in my face. Rearing back, I reclaimed my lion but lost my grip on her. She lunged, snapping at me again before whirling to run. I was on her again in an instant, biting her back leg to try to slow her down.

She spun around again, turning human mid-turn. Her gloved hand was in the dirt, and that dirt was in my eyes a moment later. I shrieked, cougar style, and reared back. It only took me a heartbeat to shake my eyes clear enough to open them again, but she was gone.

Shifting back to human, I tasted the metallic tinge of blood on my lips and wiped my sleeve across my mouth.

"Fuck!"

Chapter Eleven

I really don't remember much of the immediate aftermath.

Somehow, I wandered back out of the forest in the direction of the building. I know there were no thoughts toward stealth or hiding that I was there when I wasn't supposed to be, but I only know that because of what followed and the shreds of consciousness that managed to break through the thick, black fugue I was shrouded in.

I ran into Vance and Sam as they were taking a walk around the perimeter.

They were mad, at first. I recall some hotly spoken words, but I don't really remember the exact contents.

The anger didn't last long, though, I think.

Concern followed, it seemed. Sam picked up on there being something terribly wrong with me a little quicker than Vance did, though not by much. I think he spotted the blood on me first, though.

Questions. A lot of questions.

I looked at each of them, but their faces were blurry, and the words were incomprehensible.

"There's another one," was all I managed to say, which gave them no frame of reference or actual answer.

For more than four hundred years, I had been absolutely certain that my family had been the only ones of our kind. Multiple centuries had passed without my ever finding, meeting, or even hearing about anyone like me who I didn't already know... but there had been no mistaking the way the woman moved and shifted. No other paranormal creature could shapeshift like that. It looked different even when the fae did it or human psychics applied illusions.

She just had to be a theriomorph, but where had she come from? Who were her parents? Had one of our other siblings survived and I didn't know? Why hadn't I been able to recognize her sooner?!

As stoic and stalwart as I tried to be, losing an illusion four centuries in the making was no small hit to the psyche, and it wasn't like I'd been that grounded that night to begin with.

I could feel hands on my shoulders, and I snapped my head around to see Sam's concerned eyes looking up into mine. I could see her mouth moving, but it took a while for any of the words to actually get through to me.

"What happened?! Are you okay?"

"I..." I tried to give her an answer, but my throat constricted with a sensation I so rarely felt. Tears filled my eyes as I stared back at her, and I saw the intensity of her concern grow when she realized I was crying.

"Secure the scene," she told Vance. "I gotta take her home."

He nodded with concern of his own. "Go." He and I were practically like siblings by now, and he knew me well enough to know how frightening this reaction was.

The drive home was quiet. The tears continued. I stared out the window, watching the Adelheid countryside at night pass by. My brain felt like it was full of static, the kind that happened on cable television at three in the morning or just prior to a test of the emergency broadcast system. My tears, I knew, were just as much for the family I had lost as anything else, but the pain of the grief was a wound reopened by the idea that we—my brother and I—weren't alone. Not an island of our species. That concept had not occurred to me in so many decades that the resurgence of the idea now was physically painful.

I really was doing my best to rein it all back in, though, because I didn't like being like this. And I really didn't like other people seeing me like this.

We reached the house, and Sam took my hand as we walked in. I was functionally mute by this point from the war within me to keep my shit together.

That lasted about five minutes.

When I saw my brother, the waterworks kicked on again despite all my best efforts. I threw my arms around his neck and hugged him tightly. His body stiffened in shock, though he still hugged me back, even as he asked Sam over my shoulder what was going on. I still couldn't say anything, and Sam didn't have the answer either. Eventually, Sam managed to convince me to change into clothing that wasn't bloody and then she and my brother got me to the couch. I laid down with my head in my girlfriend's lap as my brother put a blanket over me. He had a sort of deer in the headlights look and excused himself.

Sam didn't ask any questions. We lay in the dim living room, and she rubbed my back while I stared into nothing and fought with my own psyche.

At some point, I had no idea how long, Madison walked in with my dog. Buster immediately jumped into action, leaping onto the couch and laying all sixty-someodd pounds of himself on my chest. I hugged him as he laid his blocky head against mine. A woman good at reading the room, Madison didn't ask any questions. Sam thanked her for watching Buster, and the werewolf left.

Sam's phone rang at some point. She answered it and spoke quietly, but she didn't leave me. It was Vance. My hearing could pick up his voice even though the phone was to Sam's ear.

"We entered the building shortly after you left when we heard someone scream from inside, and it's good we did," I heard him tell her. "It's...bad. We got forensics in there but also ambulances and paramedics, with Nykk and social services waiting for us at the hospital."

I felt Sam's body tense beneath my neck.

"How bad?" she asked in a low voice.

"At least a dozen victims who are still alive, all having been in cages like lab rats." I wasn't a very empathic person, but even I could hear the anger in his voice. I felt something new and icy growing in me. He went on, "They are all clearly traumatized and all had lots of physical injuries. There is a ton of high-end hunting gear in here, so I...can guess what was happening."

"Dear God..."

Im namen des Vaters... I whispered in my mind.

"We arrested about half a dozen guards, and we also brought in a man who showed up while we were here. He was decked out in hunting gear. He was screaming for a lawyer the minute he learned we were cops." He was growling words now more than speaking them, his voice dropping a couple octaves in his rage. "There is an office. We are taking everything. But there is no blue SUV, and the woman Dakota chased... Well, she's long gone."

Sam was quiet for a long moment. "Alright, thanks for the update. I'll be in the office as soon as I can."

"How's Dakota?" he asked.

My eyes were closed, but I felt her look down at me. "I'll let you know when I do." And they hung up.

I felt bad keeping her from work, but I couldn't seem to open my mouth to tell her that she could go.

I...needed her.

A little while later, Edward returned. He had Lorelai with him. I finally felt able to sit up, although Buster was less than thrilled with the change. He had to settle for curling up beside me as I looked between three silent, concerned faces. Lorelai handed me a mug, which I quickly figured out was coffee with whiskey in it. It was a small gesture that I found myself exceptionally grateful for.

I started with the basics and just spat out what happened—how I'd gone to the place and saw the woman leave from the back, I chased her, and watched her shapeshift. That the shifts were familiar to the point where I was sure that there was only one species she could be, although there was something weird about it too. Something that, in present retrospect, I just couldn't put my finger on.

Edward just stared at me with a familiar sort of...dead-eyed stare. In a rare show of demonstrative affection, we took one another's hand and squeezed. The strength in that grip would have broken the bones in a human's hands, but it was oddly grounding for people like us.

"You both know that we lost almost all our family a long time ago," I went on, "with the exception of Hannah, who was...a much more recent loss." As Sam knew...but that was otherwise a story for another time. "Our family were the only ones like us that we ever even knew existed."

"Yeah..." Edward joined in, his voice distant. "In four centuries, we were it. No one can guess where we even came from. Our DNA is enough to show that we aren't, like, aliens from outer space or something, we share the same DNA like other preternatural beings, but that's all. Where... Where could another one have come from without us having known about them in all this time, even after Cameron's Law?"

I shook my head slowly and then took a sip of the strong coffee. "I can't even begin to imagine." My voice was soft. So soft, in fact, that I could tell the human ears in the room had trouble understanding me. I repeated it and then went on. "I don't know how I couldn't have smelled the theriomorph sooner, too. I did when we were fighting. When we were really, really close, I could tell. I recognized a something to her scent that I've only found around you, or Hannah, or our family so long ago. But with my sense of smell, it should have been much sooner."

This was the first time Sam had chimed in. "Maybe it was just so unexpected that your brain didn't register it," she said. "I've seen that happen more often than you'd think."

That was a distinct possibility, I supposed, but it was still hard to wrap my mind around.

"I don't think the two of you, as much as you love us, can properly imagine what it's been like for us," Edward said, voice low and emotionally raw. "To be the only one of your species on the entire planet... To know that the only other ones who were like you are all dead. Our parents? Murdered by bigots. Three siblings? Same. One...turned totally evil and had to be taken out by ourselves, and then to leave us, in the end, as having only each other as the others of our kind."

"Yeah," I said sadly. It felt like that whole world was sitting between my shoulder blades right then. "We love you, but it isn't quite the same. You're both human. Yeah, Sam, you got some extra to the DNA, but you're still human. You're in a world full of humans."

Sam smiled faintly and put her hand on my arm. My brother still had one hand, and the other was holding a coffee mug, even though I'd already drained most of it. "I can't understand," she agreed, "but I think I get it enough to know why this was so affecting. I can't imagine knowing that this woman is tied up with all this...depravity helps either. After Hannah and all."

That drew a faint, mirthless laugh from me. "Yeah, there's that too. She fought me. She didn't seem to care that we were the same, not like I did, and got the upper hand... I have no idea how to even find her, even though I know we'll want to and for more reasons than her species."

"We'll find her," Sam said encouragingly. "After all, you always catch what you hunt, right?"

I put the empty mug on the coffee table and laid down again, my head back in her lap. "Right..."

Chapter Twelve

I didn't know how long had passed, as I must have drifted in and out of some sort of...state of shock. It was like sleep but not really? Either way, time passed.

It was still nighttime when I woke, however. The sky outside the windows was still solidly dark when Sam's cell phone rang, and she answered it. I heard Vance's voice come over the receiver a moment later. It was something about the office from the building where we'd been before. They had found some addresses of other buildings seemingly connected to the business of this one, and he was heading to search one of them.

"Are you okay if I go meet him there?" Sam asked me.

"Of course," I replied. My eyes had still been closed, but somehow, she had known I was awake.

"I'll be there in ten," Sam said into the phone and then hung up. She began to shift her body, preparing to stand, but I didn't move to let her do so just yet. One might say I was a bit of a blockhead myself, so I fairly easily kept her pinned. "I thought you said I could go."

I couldn't help a small smirk. I was feeling better

than I had earlier. "I did, and you can, but..."

Her eyes narrowed at me. I didn't look, but I could feel it. "...but?"

Shifting myself over onto my back, I finally opened my eyes and looked up at her. "I'd like to come with you."

She opened her mouth to protest instantly. "I really don't think that's a good idea—"

"I mean, maybe it's not the best idea I've ever had, but it's not the worst either," I interrupted her. "I'm feeling much better and over the shock now, and I'm involved in this case. If I'm going to help you find this woman—and we both know that you *need* me to help find this woman—then I need as much information as possible. Plus, if she appears again, you'll need my help there too. I won't be caught blindsided again."

"Dakota, I..." she began, but then she trailed off with a sigh. Her pretty gray-green eyes looked off into the shadows of the room, which was quiet since Edward and Lorelei had moved on at some point while I was sort of in-and-out. She knew I was right. And she hated that I was right, since she knew she wasn't wrong. It was one of those kinds of things. "Alright. Fine. But if you do start having some kind of...theriomorph PTSD thing, you need to back off quick. Yes, I am sure that we'll need your help, but we also need you with what wits you still maintain about you."

My brows knit for a few moments as I tried to figure out if that was a (loving) diss or not. It didn't matter. "Fine," I agreed, pushing myself to a sitting position and only then realizing that my dog wasn't on top of me anymore.

Sam read my mind. "He went to nap on a bed that didn't shift around and groan so much."

That was definitely a (loving) diss. "Fair."

We both stood up and stretched briefly after being in the same positions for so long on the sofa. After filling two travel mugs with very strong coffee, we left the house. At this point, I saw that Sam had somehow gotten someone to not only find my car where I'd left it but also had it brought home. I smiled both ruefully and gratefully in her direction, and we decided to take separate vehicles in case one needed to leave ahead of the other. With that, we were on the road.

This new location was on the opposite side of town from the last one, but it was no less deep into the dark woods. Adelheid had more than its fair share of huge tracts of forest, after all. It was the preternatural capital of possibly the United States, and much land had been bought by the newly out, free, and legal vampires who then brought in some newly out, free, and legal human earth-type psychics to encourage forest growth. There was rarely a paranormal critter in existence who didn't like some woods to disappear into...

Somehow, we arrived at the building as the same time as Vance and the other cops...or maybe he'd arrived shortly before and had waited for us. He gave me a bit of the side-eye, but he didn't say anything. We just all exchanged those silent macho nods of acknowledgement before heading in. This time, I behaved myself. I stayed in my human form and went in behind all the cops, most of whom looked ready for preternatural bear after what they had seen at the last building.

This was…not any better.

It may have, in fact, been worse.

The first thing that hit everyone, especially those with a paranormal nose, was the smell. It was somewhere between outhouse and animal pens.

The bottom level of what was clearly a two-story building was just one big space, much like a barn, full of cages and small corral-like pens.

Once through the door, though, the sounds came next. There was screaming and shrieking, both animal and human, but other sounds cut through the cacophony. There was so much sensory noise that it took everyone a moment, but then Vance—followed quickly by Sam—shot across the open space to a far corner. I followed, since I wasn't sure what else to do with myself, and we came around a corner to see something straight out of a medical/body horror movie. A surgical suite crammed into the corner of a dingy barn.

Two burly men were pinning a woman—werewolf, I thought—to the table while a third was hooking the struggling creature up to an IV. It was easy to see that nothing was flowing into the body; it was flowing out.

They were taking her blood, and she was not a willing participant.

All the cops immediately surged forward. Everything in me wanted to join them, but I was sort of a civilian in this situation and didn't want to end up as a problem in their orchestrated, trained movements. It was just a fucking mess, though, was what it was. The victim was clearly out of her mind, reminding me of that young woman in the video at the police station, and she caused almost as much issue as subduing her attackers did.

I slipped back out into the main space to try to help the others as they worked through this horror show.

Now, I could see more tables lining the back walls. There were other victims, but they were sedated. The blood was flowing. I could smell all manner of preternatural creatures here, but I couldn't really identify who was who.

Some cages were empty, smeared with blood.

Others were full of beings, catatonic or psychotic.

Some of the corrals were full too, creatures all mashed together like ill-treated cattle. I saw shapeshifters pinned against fences that were clearly threaded with silver, but they didn't care. A few were half-shifted, body parts a mix of human and different animals, sizzling where they made contact with the dangerous substance.

I turned a moment later to see a cop walking the werewolf girl out of the building. She seemed to have calmed now. Sam was nearly shouting over the noise into her cell phone that they needed to send more ambulances and transports than they had originally planned on. Vance was shouting orders, and more cops emerged with those three from the corner now in cuffs and being marched outside.

I had wanted to come, but I hadn't imagined this... How could I? I still had a soul. (I was pretty sure.) I could not have imagined something this depraved.

Sam came up beside me, and she had a haunted look in her eyes that I was pretty sure was in mine too. It seemed to be in everyone's. "This is a blood farm," I said quietly.

"My guess, specialty. These are all preternatural beings," she said. "There's a black market for specialty blood. Reports coming in over the past few months in other cities where there are request farms. Someone can ask for what they want, and someone else will go out and get it."

"My God, Sam," I whispered. "There's got to be… dozens of people here."

Two things happened simultaneously at that moment:

One, a young officer in uniform came up to us. She started to speak, right as…

Two, Vance shouted "WHAT THE FUCK?!" at vampire volume from outside the building.

The young, uniformed officer blushed faintly. "Detective Johnston has just seen what I was sent in to report," she said. The poor thing looked a little green. "There's more… Outside… In pens like animals. Like mistreated animals. And there are bodies. Out back. In…" She paused and bit her bottom lip hard enough for me to see she nearly made it bleed. "They're piled up out back."

Sam bowed her head slightly. "Thank you, Officer Lopez."

The girl went away. Sam and I stood there for just a moment. I took her hand and squeezed it gently.

"We have work to do."

I've always considered myself to be a pretty hardened bitch, right? After the life I've had and the amount of it I've had, one has to become such just to continue through the days. I had experienced a lot, so it took a lot to faze me.

This day was testing that, and how.

Dawn began to approach, so the vampires on the scene had to go home. The humans and other preternaturals continued the work, and I did so with them as best I could.

Each victim had to be pulled from their confines, but that wasn't always easy. Some were pliant because they had clearly given up or were just wildly anemic. Others had lost their minds and fought against everything and everyone. All of them had to be taken to the hospital, and some were going to need shuttling to the bigger medical facilities. Our local hospital wouldn't be able to handle this many. Social workers were being called and woken up. Nykk was on the phone frequently to get updates.

Once it was mostly light, I had to take a break. I went outside and just sat in the dirt, leaning back against a tire. I didn't care if I got dirty. I wasn't sure if I'd ever feel clean again after tonight.

Sam joined me several minutes later. It was clear she felt similarly, since she just sat down right next to me.

'Shellshocked' wasn't really a term used anymore, but it seemed to apply to the look in her eyes. "So far, we've found fourteen bodies behind the building. A couple have been there for a while. We've removed twenty-three living victims from inside, although the hospital says that a couple of them are borderline..." She was looking at her hands, and I had to wonder if some of her psychometric skills had broken through.

My girlfriend had the ability to read impressions from physical objects. It wasn't an exact science, but it could often bring interesting information...or just emotional information. She could typically block readings, so she wasn't getting impressions from everything she ever touched, but sometimes it broke through on her. I could only imagine, although I didn't want to, what impressions she had gotten from this.

I put my arm around her shoulders and pulled her against me. She took a deep breath and let it out with a shudder.

"Some of what we've gotten from them matches what we know from earlier," she went on. "There was a woman here frequently who could change her shape at will. Sometimes, it was animals. Other times, she just changed her human face. She seemed to torment them, though from afar. A few mentioned that she always wore gloves."

Unbidden, the reaction of the vampires in that shack when I shapeshifted there came to mind... I didn't linger. "She was wearing them earlier too," I commented thoughtfully. "I didn't think much of it at the time, but she had a scarf around her head. It wasn't like...a religious looking one. It was more like someone getting ready to clean. Simple leather gloves, I think."

Sam nodded slightly. "Lines up," she agreed.

"One was almost lucid and mentioned that the woman seemed to be in charge."

I groaned quietly. "Even my sister wasn't this bad," I said. "How... How does anyone get this fucked up?"

"I've asked myself that question a lot in this line of work." Sam sighed again, leaning her head on my shoulder. "I still haven't found any answers."

No one was around, so I kissed the top of her head with a long sigh of my own. What could I say? I had asked myself that often enough in the past and didn't have any better answers either.

"I'd ask how you are, but..." I began.

"Yeah," she laughed faintly. "As well as one can be, I suppose."

Sometimes, that was as much as anyone could ask for.

Chapter Thirteen

The sun was fully up by the time I finally left the scene. Sam had to stay and help with the last of the efforts, but she sent me off since there wasn't much else I could do. Truth be told, I'm not sure how much I could do while I was there, but I did try to help. It was enough of a hellscape that even my usual acerbic wit had taken a back seat to just trying to be... well, human, if we used the word lightly.

Naturally, the lights were off when I arrived home because while the sun was indeed up, it was still stupid fucking early. Even Lorelei didn't get up this early for dog caretaking.

I slipped through the door as quiet as I could, which was pretty quiet because I was good at sneaking. I grabbed an energy drink from the fridge because I thought the caffeine might distract my nerves from the night I'd had, but my adrenaline dumped right back out when I passed the living room and saw a dark figure sitting on the couch. It took me a moment, which was a moment more than my heart could handle, to realize it was my brother.

"Damn it, Erik," I said, resorting to his "before times" name when we'd been children. "You almost scared the life out of me. Haven't I had a rough enough night?"

He smiled faintly and turned on the small lamp on the side table. Why he hadn't done that before, I would never know—since I wouldn't bother asking—but it helped illuminate things a bit. My night vision was good, but even I had limits.

"I was waiting for you, Anneliese," he said. His use of my childhood name seemed a little more on purpose than my use of his, but I didn't bring it up. He gestured at the table where there was a bottle of werewolf whiskey. I had to smirk at the fact that there weren't even glasses. He knew me too well. "I thought maybe we should talk, you know, just the two of us."

Standing in the space where the hall to the bedrooms, the living room, and the kitchen all met, I contemplated if I was up to doing that. I was to the point where I couldn't even be sure of all the bullshit I'd already dealt with today. Not that talking with my brother was bullshit, most of the time, but... Well. Yeah.

I went and sat next to him on the couch, pulling the bottle toward me. I didn't tell him about where I'd been or what I'd seen or what I had been doing. He didn't need all those images to fester in his brain, too. Instead, I opened the whiskey and took a very long drink before passing it to him. He did the same. The shaggy mutts knew a thing or two about brewing a strong liquor. One glass could put the average human in a coma, but Edward and I just coughed our way through the first couple of drinks until we got used to it.

"Who do you think she is?" he finally asked.

"I wish I had the faintest idea." Sighing, I slumped into the sofa and leaned my head back. I stared at the water stain in the ceiling, which hadn't been painted over after the hole in the roof had been repaired. Idly, I thought that I should probably get around to doing that at some point, but I knew I'd forget about it the moment I got off the couch. "We have to be related to her, though, right? I mean... What are the chances that there's one other theriomorph on the planet and we aren't somehow connected."

He shrugged. "Who knows? I mean, we don't even know if that's what we're called."

That was a point, I thought. Our parents had never named our species, except in a few off-hand sort of references, but those words were in German and didn't quite have direct English translations. The term theriomorph had actually come about after Cameron's Law and the legal process. In fact, it was kind of my fault. I was the only one of my kind to come forward at the time, and that demographic box on the form had to be filled with something. I dragged up some terminology from the folklore on the internet and just went with it.

Still, name or not, we knew what we were.

"Mama and Papa couldn't have known of any others," he went on. "I mean, they would have mentioned something about there being others, wouldn't they?"

"I'd like to think so," I agreed, "but who can say? If they knew but didn't tell us, there was probably a good reason." I thought about it for a few moments, taking another drink without even lifting my head. It wasn't a great angle or trajectory down my throat, but I did it anyway. "What if they were, like...evil? I mean, the one I fought tonight has been in charge of some..." Even I hesitated with how to say this. "...really, really ugly things."

He sighed. "I hope you can find her," he said. "Because I'd like to know if she has some answers."

"I'm going to find her," I said. "Because she has a lot to answer for."

Since it was hardly unusual for me to go to sleep after the sun was up, that wasn't a problem. I took Buster for a quick outing first, once he woke up when I walked into the bedroom, and then he and I settled in for as much of a "night's" sleep as I could get.

Unfortunately, it turned out to not be much. The number of hours wasn't terrible, but I was restless. There were dreams, but I couldn't remember them upon waking...which was both good and bad. It still fucked up my mood, but I had less understanding of where the mood fuckery came from. At least when I remembered the dream, I knew what the culprit was and could be grumpy with specificity.

I dragged myself out of bed sometime in the afternoon and drank about half a pot of coffee before I felt cognizant. I took the dog for a walk, although I didn't go far from the house...not after the last time. That thought was still too fresh, despite everything that had followed.

While standing in the yard, listening to all the other dogs on the property barking and waiting for Buster to make his circuit, I pulled my cell phone from my pocket and called Sam. She answered on the third ring, and for a moment, I worried that I had woken her, but I learned she was out getting a coffee while running a couple of errands before work. I had to imagine that she couldn't have gotten much sleep.

"How're you doing?" I asked, because I was concerned. That had been a lot for anyone, and she'd done even more than I had with even less downtime to recover.

"About as you'd expect," she replied wryly. "I'm going to be surviving on caffeine and spite today and not much else."

"I've managed to live four centuries that way." This earned a quiet laugh. "Maybe try to catch a nap in the breakroom."

"I just might." She then paused and thanked someone, which I assumed was not for me but rather someone at a drive-thru window before she went back to me. "You get any sleep?"

My first response was a sort of noncommittal grunt. My more elaborate response was, "Not enough, but some, so I'll make do." I waited for a moment before letting my curiosity get the better of me. "How'd the rest of the night go?"

"Not much to report," she said. I could hear passing traffic. She must have been pulling out onto the road. I'd have busted her for talking on a cell phone while driving, which wasn't legal in this state, but I knew she had a wireless setup. She was a good girl, after all. "Everyone who was alive went to the hospital, spread out over three of them. Seems like every social worker and victim's advocate in the state has been mobilized. The bodies were brought to the morgue, which also saw a few sent to another location, so we can try to identify them. So far, no one sent to a hospital has been lost, but I hear at least two are still borderline."

I hoped they'd pull through. I wasn't normally a 'bleeding heart' type, but one couldn't be without compassion here. They had all clearly already been through so much that I didn't want to see anything worse befall them.

We moved on to a bit of related chatter. I heard her reach the station and get out of her car. After the door shut, I moved on to my next point. "I was thinking it could be useful to go back to that first building," I went on, "the one where I first saw the woman and check it out again now that it's clear. Would it be okay if me and Edward did that? I could use his nose along with me." He and I had sometimes hunted together; he could be useful.

Sam sounded a little reluctant, but I figured it was because of what happened there last night. She probably didn't want it upsetting me, but we all had a job to do, and the stakes were rapidly getting higher. Edward being with me actually seemed to ease her slightly, despite his being a not-really-professional.

"Just be careful, okay?" she said.

"Promise."

It didn't take much effort to convince my brother to go with me. Lorelei looked a little worried in the same way I imagined Sam had been, but she didn't argue with us.

We made short work of the drive back to the

turnoff, where I parked my car with a small prayer that someone wouldn't come and tow the damn thing. I knew there was an actual driveway up to the building, but I had yet to learn where that was since I always seemed to come to this building in some sort of clandestine way.

"So, they were using this place as a staging ground for hunting...people?" Edward asked with a deep frown as we started into the trees. Although I'd kept a lot of information from him about this case, I did have to explain some of what we'd found here so he could help me search.

We reached the electrified fence, which I had also told him about so we both shifted into the smallest forms we could in order to pass under it.

The device would be a good deterrent against almost any other species, given that shapeshifters took too long to shift for a sudden swerve. I doubted they took ones with bird forms for something like this, or they'd just fly away...unless they had something else that kept them in the confines of this compound. I couldn't know, and I wasn't sure that I really even wanted to know.

"That's what it seems to be," I agreed once we were back in human form. Even though I already knew that the police had cleared this area out, I was still wary and watchful as we moved. "They had a bunch of different preternatural creatures penned up like animals and all kinds of hunting gear. A dude dressed in it even showed up while they were here. Last I heard, he was down at the police station. This is kind of illegal and all."

"And this theriomorph woman was running it?"

"Seems to be," I repeated. I didn't know anything for sure, but I knew what the evidence we had so far suggested. I kept the fact that she also seemed to use her abilities to torment the victims further to myself.

When we reached the building, we made a quick circuit to see if anyone was still there or had come back after the cops left, but we found it just as deserted as it was supposed to be. There was some crime scene tape and markers set out, but we avoided all of those and moved around to the side of the building where I'd seen the woman come out.

From there, we shifted into animal forms with better noses than the human forms and set to work.

I could pick up on her scent easily enough at the door, though I realized it was mingling with my own and confused certain areas that we moved over. There was only one track, so Edward and I moved side-by-side. We moved into the trees, and then to the space where the woman and I had fought. That was evident by some blood droplets and compressed foliage. I remembered where I'd been standing and then shifted to where I recalled her being. Edward and I were able to follow the trail for a little while, but it didn't last long after the fight.

"Bird," I said, shifting back to human once we'd circled the area and determined that the scent was gone. It didn't surprise me, but I'd been holding out some hope that she hadn't taken wing.

We spent a little more time sniffing around the whole building, and we found several trails—of varying ages—that spoke to her presence here. We didn't go inside, because I knew that was still a sealed crime scene, but we didn't find anything more outside that would actually lead us to the woman. It had been a long shot, I knew, but every hunt started somewhere. Usually at the beginning, and since this was where I learned what the woman was, this was the beginning for me now.

With that, we headed back to the car. I felt... heavy, but I didn't know that there was much of anything for it.

Edward seemed to pick up on this, though, and nudged me a little. "Wanna race?"

I looked at him with a sidelong smirk. "Say what?"

"A race," he said just before we shifted small, crawled under the fence, and stood up again as humans. "A race like only our kind can, y'know? Only rule is no birds."

For a long moment, I looked at him like he had just lost his mind, but his expression told me that he was trying to cheer me up, so I relented. "Fine," I said with a small laugh, realizing that he was probably right. A little life, a little familial love, had to help... "First one back to the car is the winner."

He nodded once. "What does the loser have to do?"

"Buy the next bottle of whiskey?"

"Bottle of werewolf whiskey and fae nectar wine."

"...and handle vacuuming the dog hair for the next week."

"Deal."

"Deal."

"Go!"

CHAPTER FOURTEEN

By the time we got back to the car, we were both covered in brambles and leaves. I had to give it to Edward, however. It had cheered me a bit. We drove home and helped Lorelei take care of the dogs, and then we sat down and had a late dinner like civilized people. It wasn't something we did often, and it felt a little weird to act like we should be on a 1950s family TV show, but it was also kind of nice. Especially since I hadn't cooked, which meant it was edible.

After dark had fallen, I decided to head over to Adelheid's Coven House. This was the seat of the town's vampire coven, so if anyone would have an ear for what was going on with the town's vampires, this was the place to go.

Of course, I called ahead. I wasn't usually subject to an excess of politeness, but Jade—the coven leader—was a powerful vampire and a woman who commanded respect. I had done a little work for her here and there over the past few years, and I knew that she wasn't fond of surprises. So, I called. She said I could come visit her that night, and I hopped in my car and drove over immediately. No time like the present and all that.

Although, it wasn't a concern that she wouldn't be there. I'm not sure if she ever actually left the Coven House. I wasn't going to ask.

When I arrived, I was greeted by the lead warden, Shayna. She was nearly as tall as I was and had been a member of the Israeli Mossad before she was turned into a vampire. She emitted all the aura that someone tasked with defending the heart of vampire life in Adelheid would be expected to give off. Most people were instantly intimidated by her, but not me. Few people actually intimidated me, especially if I wasn't dating them.

A woman of few words, she inclined her head and led me into the sitting room. I sat and waited, but I didn't have to wait too long before Jade walked in.

Where Shayna was nearly six feet tall and corded with lean muscle, Jade was just a smidge over five and delicately slender. She was Asian, although I'm not sure I'd ever learned where she was originally from five centuries ago. Every movement and gesture was economical and measured in that creepy way vampires had. She smiled politely and then sat in the large armchair beside the couch I was on.

"Thanks for seeing me," I said, feeling the way I always did around her—like a hulking brute. I briefly considered shifting into a smaller human form, but I didn't.

"Of course," she replied smoothly. "I assume it's something of great importance, given you are not one for social calls."

I chuckled faintly. She had me there. "It's part of a case I'm working for the cops, yeah," I said, pausing to weigh just how much information I should give out. "I was wondering if you've heard of anything about... blood farms here in Adelheid."

One dark brow rose on her face, and she tilted her head slightly. "Naturally, the coven has a couple of farms ourselves," she began, "but they are like any other farm. We use animals, and of course we treat them...humanely." She paused with subtle but apparent amusement at using that word for something vampires did. "I sense that it's not this sort of farm you are inquiring about."

"I'm afraid not. The one I mean is...less humane," I said carefully. "I think the word Sam used was 'specialty' blood."

Jade nodded slowly, her face somber. "I have begun to hear...rumors, although I don't know anything concrete. They have thus far been rumors only, and if any of my vampires here have taken part, I do not know of it. I feel like if a vampire living here were partaking, however, I would have caught wind of it. Abby may have sensed something."

Abby, short for Abilene, was a vampire who lived in the Coven House. Two thousand years old trapped in the body of a pre-adolescent and the creepiest thing you've ever met. That would be a story for some other time, though.

"Could you keep an ear out for me?" I asked. "It seems that someone has been running one of these farms in our town, but they aren't willing subjects."

Even though her face was generally impassive, not wasting energy on extravagant expressions, I could see a stormy sort of darkness in her black eyes.

She inclined her head once. "I will certainly do so," she agreed. "This sort of thing is an affront, and it reflects poorly on my species and those of us who are in this city."

I nodded. "Thank you, Jade. I appreciate it."

The visit had been short, and I'd managed to get out without having to see the creepy one. It hadn't reaped much of a reward, but maybe it would with a little more time.

I was already exhausted. My preternatural stamina was flagging now, and I reflected on the past... Was it only twenty-four hours? Maybe thirty-six. I was sure it hadn't even been two full days, at least, and all that had happened... There was still so much to do, and try to do, but I needed to take a moment.

There was something else that needed to be done, I realized in a random moment of clarity.

First things first, I went home.

I needed to take Buster out, and after that, I piled him into my car with me. The big goof was a fan of car rides, so convincing him to jump in wasn't difficult. He didn't care where we went, as long as I opened the window so he could stick his big head out of it. Even in the winter. He could be a baby about the cold and the snow, but apparently, neither of those counted if it was felt through the window of a car.

We drove to Sam's apartment building. I didn't call, though I wasn't sure why. Instead, we went to the door and knocked, but no joy. I took Buster for a walk around the building. The pair of us wasn't a totally unfamiliar sight, so it wasn't like I worried about the neighbors causing me any trouble. And being so close to a hive of population, being an apartment building complex, I felt reasonably sure that I wouldn't be seeing any blue SUVs sidling up beside me.

The pup and I did make it to the convenience store right on the corner, set beside the furthest apartment building in the cluster. He hung out at a lamp post outside while I popped in and grabbed a few snacks, for me and the dog and Sam. We walked back to my girlfriend's place and sat ourselves down outside her door. We broke into the treats while waiting, and happily, we didn't even get through them all before Sam arrived home. (I was fully prepared to eat hers as well if she took too long.)

She looked surprised, briefly, to see us.

"You weren't attacked again, were you?" she asked with genuine concern.

I smirked as I got to my feet. "Thankfully, no," I replied, then my expression flattened a little. "I just wanted to see you. I wanted to talk." I held the bag up. "I brought snacks."

That made her chuckle as she stepped past me to unlock and open the door. "Might as well come in, then," she said.

Her place was a fairly quintessential 'bachelor pad' where the bachelor just happened to be a bachelorette. It was a one bedroom, with the bedroom being just a few steps up from glorified closet. The kitchen was pretty much a hallway, and then every other sort of living area—except the bathroom, of course—was in the remaining space. She wasn't a slob by any means, but she wasn't a neat freak either, so I was hardly surprised to see a few coffee cups loitering on the counter next to the sink and a few layers of sweatshirts over the back of the sofa.

She grabbed a couple paperbacks from the couch cushion and put them on the coffee table. Buster, naturally, assumed this was an invitation. He jumped up into the corner, curled up, and seemingly went to sleep in an instant. Even I couldn't fall asleep that fast.

"So, what did you want to talk about?" she asked as she took out the coffee carafe and checked the contents. Determining it to be a lost cause, she tossed the remnants in the sink and starting making more. "Not that there isn't plenty going on that needs talking about. I'm just curious which one is the choice of the moment."

Normally, I appreciated how she could get straight to the point. At that exact instant, it just made me feel more awkward. As literally anyone who had ever met me could attest, 'emotional stuff' (unless the emotion was anger) was not my best area.

"I, ah..." I began, fidgeting with the paper bag with the snacks, taking them out and placing them on the counter to hide as much of my mental flailing as I could. "I know I've been weird lately."

"Well, someone did try to kidnap you," she offered. "And then you had an earth-shattering discovery, and then we visited a hell house..."

These were all solid points, and they were also beside the one I was trying to make. "I meant before that."

"Ah, that."

"Yeah, that..."

I stalled out a little there. She finished getting the coffee going and turned to face me, leaning back against the counter and folding her arms across her chest. She didn't push, but she just looked at me. And waited.

"It was the news that my brother is gonna have a baby, okay?" The words rapid-fired themselves out of me quicker than I usually spoke.

I looked at her and saw she was smirking a little.

"I'm pretty sure Lorelei is the one having the baby," she said.

Anyone else, I might think they were mocking me. Sam? She was breaking the tension of the moment, and it worked. I laughed and shook my head. She took my hand and led me to the couch. It wasn't a very long piece of furniture, so we had to sit close in the room that Buster had left to us. That was okay, though.

"Okay, now, tell me why that's been a problem," she said, resting her legs over my lap and putting her elbow on the couch back, leaning her head on her hand.

"I just... I don't know." I really didn't want to admit it. "It got me weird, though I wasn't really sure why at first. You know analyzing my feelings is hardly my best skill." She was kind enough to not reply to that. "I guess I suddenly got worried that you...might... want a kid someday and...leave me." I squeezed my eyes shut at confessing all that.

The silence rolled on for way too long, which made me open my eyes and look at her again. She looked a little dumbfounded, but then she started laughing. "Anneliese," she said, as one of the few to know and be allowed to use that name, "you're an idiot."

That was unexpected. I didn't even find an immediate reply, so she continued.

"Look, okay, I suppose I can see the concern. But you know that I grew up as one of six kids, for fuck's sake. Six kids and one bathroom. Life was chaos on ridiculous levels. I don't want that! I like my job, for one, and it isn't ideal for having a family, especially on the baby-carrying side of it. I like the freedom to do what I want when I want. I have always liked that your career was important to you too. I've never wanted a baby. And, God, if for some reason, I should wake up one day and have this urgent need to create a family, it's the twenty-first century! I don't need you to get me pregnant to make that happen. There are plenty of options." She laughed and shook her head. "But that's only if you wanted it too. I think after everything we've been through already, we're good for the long haul. Whatever that looks like for us. I am absolutely not going to leave you 'cause I want to find some man to knock me up."

"Well, when you put it like that," I admitted sheepishly.

She took my face in her hands and forced me to meet her eyes. "I love you, so stop worrying. And stop being an idiot."

I never thought I'd like being called an idiot twice in ten minutes so much.

CHAPTER FIFTEEN

I woke up the next day feeling like my chest was being crushed. For a moment, I thought I was having a heart attack, until I felt the snoring reverberating against my skull. I realized that Buster was sleeping on top of me...but even that hadn't been what woke me up.

There was this loud, electronic song-like noise coming from the nightstand. It wasn't my phone. It was Sam's.

She groaned beside me and crawled up from under the blankets, reaching her unclothed body across me to grab it. She squinted at the caller ID and then answered it. Around the sound of my dog, who I had no idea when he'd even gotten into the bed since it was after we'd fallen asleep, I heard her talking with some of the cops working the day shift. That meant it wasn't Vance, since his vampire ass was in a sunlight coma.

"We've been following up on the information found in the office of the first building," I heard the man report. She didn't have it on speaker or anything. My hearing was just that good, in spite of the dog. "We found another address and have visited the location."

"What did you find?" Sam asked. I could hear the reluctance in her voice. She had to know, but she didn't want to know.

"This one, ah..." The guy sounded bothered. Even I could tell that much. "This one looks like some kind of science lab. We are working through the scene. The computer is locked down better than the other ones, so the techs are working on cracking it open, but our best guess is...some sort of experiments. It looked like something out of *Frankenstein*...or *The Island of Dr. Moreau*."

I appreciate the literary knowledge, even if I didn't like the imagery.

"Are there people there?" Sam continued.

"No dead ones here," he said, "but eleven living ones who are just as much of a mess as the other ones we've found. They're all on their way to whichever hospitals have space for them. Every ER and psych unit is getting run thin. They're even saying they may bring in some folks from out of state, if they have to. I mean, it's not just the trauma, but there is some specialized care for the preternaturals with the silver wounds and poisoning."

Sam rubbed her eyes. "What a mess," she said quietly.

I could practically hear the guy nodding. "Yes, sir," he agreed. "We are still identifying addresses and will keep you apprised."

"Thanks. Good luck."

She hung up with a sigh and put the phone back on the nightstand. After rubbing her face a few more times and then using both hands to push her hair back, she looked at me with a faint, cheerless smile. "Well, good morning."

I returned the expression as best I could. Despite the news that had just come over the line, I felt better—on a personal level—after our talking and making up last night. Angling around Buster's blocky head, she kissed my cheek. "I'm going to make some coffee," she said. "Some very, very strong coffee." She slid out from under the blankets and off the bed. "That stuff I made last night is already done." We hadn't been interested in coffee after our chat. "But I still have some of that fae stuff you got me for my birthday. I feel like this kind of start to the day warrants it."

Once she was gone, I tried to take a deep breath, but...dog.

"Okay, buddy," I began, "you need to move."

He didn't.

"Buster."

Snore.

I knew I could just pick him up and move him, but that tended to make him uncomfortable. This was also an awkward angle, so I had to take a moment to think of how to get out of this position without either of us getting grumpy or wounded. Eventually, I decided on a slow-roll over to my side, which dumped him a little unceremoniously onto the spot Sam had just vacated. He snorted his disagreement with the plan but then rolled onto his other side and went back to sleep.

Two cups of coffee and one shower later, Sam and I headed out.

Work was starting early today.

We took separate cars so I could drop Buster off at home, but I went straight to the police station after that.

Sam was already in the thick of it by the time I walked into the squad room. She had the phone pressed between her shoulder and ear, since the station still used landlines with cords, even, but she saw me and waved me over. She hung up a few moments later and smiled tiredly. "Am I too young to retire?"

"I'm four hundred and still working."

If looks could kill...

"Any updates?" I moved us right on before she could get annoyed with me after we just sorted our shit out.

"Nothing since the call earlier," she said, sighing and putting her hands on her hips as she turned to look at her desk, which was covered with folders and papers, plus the computer monitor with what looked to be four different programs and thirteen tabs open already. That was never a good start to the day.

I nodded a little. "I was thinking on the drive over," I continued, "that if I could get the addresses of the locations you've found out so far from the offices that have been raided, it might help me get an idea of where this woman may run to ground or other places she may be at."

Sam grabbed the computer mouse and clicked between a few different windows. A minute later, she walked over to the squad room printer and grabbed the papers there.

First was something obviously not hers, and she

hollered for the owner to come get it. They did so, a bit sheepishly, and then Sam handed the remaining papers to me. "This is what we have found so far. It includes the actual, physical address of the place you initially found the woman at plus the other location you told us about. Again, this time, it's the addresses rather than the bass ackwards ways you got into them." I could tell she wasn't really mad about that anymore, though. "I included what little we have dug up so far about each property, too."

I took the paper from her and looked over the addresses, and then I pulled a paper map out of my back pocket. Sam opened her mouth, which I knew was her about to tease me for being so "old-fashioned," but she didn't get a chance to say it because the phone on her desk rang. That meant she had to answer it, and I smirked at my saved-by-the-bell moment.

It wouldn't last, of course, but while she talked to the next in the long line of calls she had to deal with these days, I turned to a table that was mostly clear and unfolded the map of Adelheid. I grabbed a pen from Sam's desk and began marking off the locations from the printout. I wanted to see if there was a pattern, and the actual visual—a physical thing I could look at—would help me do that.

Digital everything was useful in so many ways, but sometimes, the physical means were more useful. Or maybe it was just 'cause I was older than dirt. Either way.

After I marked the last one, Sam walked back over to me. "The chief said that we will hire you officially to help track this woman down," she said. "We are spread so thin right now, and even more so with everything we've been finding. It's all making more sense, though. All the people going missing and weird things going on that stretched us thin in the first place seem to be adding up in this disaster. As such, though, we're still having to deal with it..."

"You don't have to pay me," I said, shaking my head while still looking at my map. "This one is on the house. I need to do this for me, even if doing it for you is a happy byproduct." I smiled faintly sidelong at her.

"Alright," she said after a moment. She looked like she wanted to argue with me, but I appreciated that she didn't. She took a long breath in and then nodded to the map. "So, are the archaic ritual marks telling you anything?"

I snorted. "Yes, actually. If this woman is indeed the top boss of all this, and I am willing to bet she is, then this tells me that she is...smart but also bold." I gestured to some of the marks. "These are all well-hidden placements, deep in each forest tract, but also abutted against either public or corporate-held lands. But..." I thought of something and pulled out my phone, doing a quick search, and I snort-laughed again. "That explains so much... I tracked one of these pieces of land to a corporation run by a guy who seemed like a shadow. He's just a shell.

"According to what you have here—" I held up the paper in one hand. "—and what I can see from my own sources—" I held up the phone in the other. "—the pieces of land are privately owned or corporation-owned, with corporate lands alongside private tracts. The corporation seems to be the place I found with the shadow leader. That's just a front created by this woman, has to be. I'm going to bet we'll find businesses incorporated within businesses and a hell of a mire to try to find the real owner, who will be... this woman. Like any good shapeshifter who doesn't want to be found, she's hiding in plain sight."

Chapter Sixteen

Sam had more work to do, and so did I. For my part, I had a lot to think about.

There were bits and pieces of information aligning, and yet not all of them had come together yet. With everything that had happened, I had almost completely forgotten my brief life as a squirrel outside that parking garage trying to catch wind of a man that I was now certain didn't exist. It made sense, though.

All preternatural beings who had lived enough life before Cameron's Law had learned all sorts of ways to exist in a world that didn't know them while hiding what they were. Some of them, like this shapeshifting bitch, had learned how to use that to hide her evil deeds as well. My sister and the ancient vampire she'd aligned herself with had managed to do something similar, but I had cut through all of the bullshit then and I could do so again now.

There was no point in wondering why someone turned evil, or if they were just born that way, so I wasn't worried about that, even if this woman was a theriomorph and might hold answers to a lot of questions I had about my own existence.

Now, I just knew that this all circled around her.

I had to find her.

While Sam stayed at the station to keep doing her own job and work through the sites, finding and helping the victims, I went home to mull on my deep thoughts. The image of the theriomorph woman was foremost in my mind. Solving that puzzle would solve the rest. I just knew it. All I had at the moment, however, was my brief combative interaction with her. There was still something about that, however, that was bugging me. It was elusive trying to put my finger on what it was.

Once back at my house, I took care of Buster, although half my brain was fighting through this.

I started thinking about the attempted kidnapping, while I sat beside my dog as he ate his dinner. Had that been specifically orchestrated because the woman had spotted me in the trees that first time, or was it just happenstance that they targeted preternaturals and I was one? I would only know if I was able to get ahold of her and ask, but thinking about it did put me on the right track to untangling the first knot.

The woman was a shapeshifter just like me except...not. I realized that it was the animals she had changed into which had been bothering me. It wasn't the specific animals she chose; it was their appearance. All shapeshifting beings (except the fae, but they're just weird) turned into larger versions of any animal they chose. Maybe not always by a lot, but still bigger than average, as well as stronger and faster, because of the paranormal abilities. I hadn't been able to give it much thought at the time, but I realized that the animal forms this woman took were normal animals, maybe even smaller. The speed and strength was enough to get out from my grip the first time, but I blamed that on the shock.

What would make a shifter's forms different like that, though?

While I was trying to find that next answer, Edward and Lorelei came in. Given the time of day, I figured they had been out feeding the dogs. Our little canine rescue seemed to be getting bigger all the time, but they had started bringing in some volunteers to help with it all. Lorelei still kept her eye on things, however, since this place was her baby...

I supposed it was soon going to be 'one of' her babies.

"Hey," she said with a smile for me. "How are you feeling?"

I returned the expression, a little more genuinely than I had been lately. "I'm alright," I said. "I'm sorry if I've been a bitch lately. You know, more than usual."

My brother smirked. "Not really more than usual, no."

"You've been fine," my much-nicer sister-in-law said.

"And how're you?" I nodded pointedly at her, ignoring Edward. He made a little grumbly sound in his throat but didn't say anything otherwise.

"Oh, I'm fine too," she said, waving one hand before resting it on her stomach. "Although I think I'm feeling things further along than I'd have expected. Then again, I never could have imagined what it would be like to carry a half-preternatural baby."

My brain stopped cold.

"A..." I began, then stopped, blinking.

They both looked at me with concern, probably wondering if I was having a stroke or a seizure or something with the way I stopped mid-sentence and just stared blankly.

"Yes, a...half-preternatural baby," Edward said, waving a hand in front of my face. "You knew this."

I slapped his hand away. "Yes, I knew this, but I just figured something out!"

The woman was only *half*-theriomorph.

Now I knew this was a possibility. It explained why I didn't smell her sooner, because her paranormal scent wasn't as strong. The smaller animal forms... It wasn't a lot of evidence, no, but somehow, it just made everything make sense.

The difference was in her DNA. That was probably why the headscarves and gloves. She didn't want to leave her DNA anywhere because it was unique...

DNA!

I shot up from where I sat on the floor. My brother called after me, but I didn't reply. I just dove into my room. Buster ran after me, making little woof sounds like we were playing. I threw myself onto my bedroom floor and tossed around the pieces of laundry scattered there. Damn, I was a slob, but thank goodness for that because I still had the shirt.

I had bitten that woman and wiped her blood off on my sleeve. I had her DNA.

CHAPTER SEVENTEEN

Despite my brother still calling after me in confusion, I had raced back out of the house like a crazy woman to get my dirty shirt down to the police lab. They knew me enough down there to not balk, although they did seem a little...wary of me and my rapid-fire explanation of what I needed. I knew they would be calling Sam to make sure it was okay to proceed, and I also knew that she would give them the go-ahead.

They sent me on my way pretty quickly, though, since running such tests would not happen in an instant.

This left me back in thinking-and-planning stage, but my mind was still racing through everything I had started putting together. It could be like this sometimes, a variation on "hurry up and wait," just all in my own head. Even so, it did seem like everything had been happening very fast. Many things overlapping...but life was often just like that. It always seemed to be like that. "Life isn't one damn thing after another; the damn things overlap." I couldn't remember where I'd first heard that, but it seemed to fit so I kept it in mind.

After dark, I received a phone call. It was Jade.

"I have some information for you," she said. "We caught wind last night of some...well, let us call them less than reputable vampires in the area. Some in town and some in neighboring towns. None of them are of the Adelheid Coven, of course, as I would not tolerate such things, but we were able to find some rumors to follow. Under Shayna's...persistence, they were willing to tell us about one of the illicit farms that sells this 'specialty' blood."

I wondered if it was one of the ones that had been in the information the police had, but still, the customers were another piece to any criminal enterprise. With illicit goods, there were the sellers and the buyers. We had the sellers already, at least some of them...

Jade was still talking while my brain ran around. "...are apparently entire parties around these special goods." Although her tone was stoic and her emotions well-contained, it was impossible to miss her disgust. Whatever some of the more bigoted folks thought, there were many very moral vampires who never took blood from an unwilling sentient being. "Shayna, as convincing as she is, was able to get a name for you. Someone who is due to attend one of these parties and is in charge of picking up the blood. It's happening tonight."

"Tonight?!" I repeated with surprise. That didn't give me much time to plan anything, but I knew I couldn't just sit on the lead.

"Indeed," Jade replied, back to her usual unflappable self. She gave me the information they had, which was the name and where this person lived.

It did occur to me, briefly, if I should ask just how far Shayna's 'persistence' went, but then I thought about what I had seen in that building. I thought about all those who had died, and I thought about the young woman who might never regain her mind...and all the others who might not either, if they even survived. I thought about the man who held a gun in my face and hurt my dog. Maybe this one vampire didn't know what was going on behind the special substance he was picking up, but it was all so clandestine that he had to know something was very off about it all.

Ignorance as an excuse only went so far.

"Thank you, Jade," I said before my thoughts got too far away from me again.

"Of course," she replied. "If anything should come of this that might affect my coven, please do let me know?"

"Of course," I echoed, and we hung up.

I looked at the small notepad that I had written the name and address on. I knew the apartment building, although the name was unfamiliar. It wasn't anyone I could recall meeting, but there were thousands of people who lived in Adelheid. I could hardly know them all...especially as anti-social as I usually was.

Looking out the window, I thought it through. It hadn't been dark for very long, so this fella probably hadn't set out yet. If I hurried, I might just catch him...

He was a pasty, spindly little vampire creature. I didn't even want to think of him by any name. He was young, I could tell that much. The scent of the grave was very faint on him, and he was clearly just waking up by the time I arrived. That meant he couldn't shake off the daylight coma as early or as easily as older vampires could. Maybe his age had something to do with his lack of thinking things through...or maybe he just didn't have any morals before becoming a vampire.

I wasn't going to work hard to find out.

The moment he stepped out of his door, I was laser-focused on following him. I shifted into a household cat, since I knew my usual mountain lion self certainly would not blend in with this neighborhood. Standing out was the exact opposite of what I wanted to do in that moment. Stealth was the name of the game right then, so I became a black cat who trotted at a reasonable distance behind this disreputable young vampire.

He got in his car, and I took on a pair of wings. Inwardly grousing at having to fly, since I really didn't enjoy it, I was able to follow his vehicle in the dark. He stayed on backroads, which meant driving slowly, and that helped me keep up without undue exertion.

The drive wasn't far, and I realized that this location had not been on the list. Once the car was parked, I dropped to the ground and shifted back into my housecat form. I knew there was a small risk for being caught out if that woman was here, but I had a strong feeling that she wouldn't be. This would be too much of a risk for her now as well, as locations were being found out and raided, plus her tussle with me would have her on alert.

I watched the young man walk up to the building and knock on the door. I sat down and observed. I was actually a little surprised that these other locations hadn't gone into lockdown, but maybe they didn't have that sort of system in place... That was to my benefit, so I wasn't going to complain. Instead, I watched as the door opened and a hulking fella who was clearly a guard gave the vampire a cooler.

Seriously? A drinks cooler? Something about that just seemed...insulting, given what others had to sacrifice to provide it.

The vampire gave the guard something, which had to be money, and they parted ways without either having crossed the threshold of the door. It was like a drive-thru for illegal blood.

I turned and trailed the vampire back to his car, where I snuck up behind him. He sensed me on some level and spun around, but he didn't realize I was so close to the ground. His eyes were still at person-level when I shapeshifted right up into his face.

Grabbing the back of his neck, while he was frozen in surprise, I smacked the back of his head into the roof of the car, hard, two or three times. I knew it wouldn't kill him, but vampires could be knocked out if you knew what you were doing.

He crumbled at my feet. I pulled my special zip ties from my pocket and wrapped them around his wrists and ankles. These were special, too, since they had little symbols engraved into the plastic that would keep him from using his vampire strength to bust out of them. If he woke up before I got back. Once he was trussed up appropriately, I opened the door to his own car's back seat and put him in.

There was something I needed to do before we

left.

I slunk my way back to the building, watching it for about ten minutes before I saw the door open. A guard stepped out. It wasn't the same as the one who'd made the exchange with the vampire, but that was fine. This one was just stepping out to have a cigarette. Wrinkling my nose, I tried to ignore the smell, but it was hard. I had a lot of bad habits, but smoking anything had never been among them. I wasn't a fan of smoke.

Maybe it was that whole family being burned alive thing...

Even so many years later.

Ignoring that part of things, I forced myself to take a deep breath and try to recognize what was what behind the smoke. As best I could tell, this one was a shifter... Werewolf, probably. I thought I picked up on something canine, and statistically speaking, a wolf was the most likely. Vampires and werewolves made up a large majority of the preternatural population. He looked young as well. I supposed both traits made sense. Regular humans wouldn't be able to handle the species they were holding captive, and the young ones were probably easier to manipulate...

I was counting on that to work in my favor, as well.

He wasn't a very good guard, I determined, since I was able to sneak up on him rather easily. All it took was a return to my housecat form and a meandering path in his direction. I was almost on top of him before he even noticed me in the first place, and then he looked at me with something like bemusement while he kept smoking. I went so far as to rub up against his legs, even if it felt gross, but I played the cat role well... right up until the moment I turned back into myself.

The man's eyes widened until I thought his eyelids might just stretch off his face, and I smiled in that...not really a smile kind of way before I grabbed his face with one hand, covering his mouth and squeezing his jaw.

"Not a word," I said, my voice low and dangerous.

It took me a moment to realize that my style of change had probably gotten the jump on him before my hired-killer vibe did since I bet all of the employees had seen that bitch's tormentor routine. That pissed me off for somewhat hypocritical reasons, but it didn't mean I wasn't going to use it to my advantage anyway.

Using his face, I pulled him away from the building and back into the trees. Out of the line-of-sight of any of the windows so that he and I could have a nice little chat.

"I need to know some information about your boss," I said simply, holding his gaze with my own unblinking one. "You know what I am. I can tell. So you also know that it's not a good idea to piss me off. I can promise that I won't tell her who told me, but I will also promise that if you tell anyone about me, I'll come back and find you. I'm a hunter, you see, and I always catch my prey." I smiled with lots of malicious teeth, snapping them in his face just once. "Got it?"

He squeaked behind my hand, nodding like he was trying to break his own head off.

I could work with that.

About an hour later, the police had two new friends with their own special jewelry.

"What..." Sam asked as she came outside the station to meet me outside a car that wasn't my own. On the back seat were two zip-tied, unconscious men. Her pale eyes swung between the two of them and then to me. "I don't need to arrest you for assault or anything, do I?"

"Of course not," I replied with A Look. I pointed to the vampire. "That one was buying illegal blood products. I watched him do it at one of those blood farms, which incidentally wasn't on the list. I'll write the address down." I pointed to the guard. "And that one worked there. I didn't go in on a Chuck Norris style one-man mission or anything. I just grabbed that guy to get some information from him. He was about to piss his pants, but aside from the headache the vampire will have and the adrenaline hangover the other will have, they are both just fine. But also criminals. So I brought them to you, gift-wrapped and all."

"We really need to work on your gift-giving skills," she commented, but she managed a small smile for me just before she hurried back into the building to grab some officers to take the two men. "We'll impound the car for now as well. I can get someone to take you home...or wherever it is that you've left your car this time."

"That would be appreciated."

Once on the road, both when I wasn't driving and when I was, I thought over what I had gotten out of that guard. He hadn't known much direct information since he was really just a lowly peon on the ladder of business, but even those at the bottom always had some information tumble toward them. He wasn't able to give me a home address, of course, but he had heard a few things that I knew I could capitalize on...if they were accurate. I just had to start there and hope they were.

He'd heard that she lived in a house, because she couldn't stand much noise being around her. Apartment buildings were out because she'd have to listen to people in apartments beside or above her. For that same reason, the house was in a rural area. Of course, in Adelheid, that was most of the houses. He did know that she had only been in town for less than two years, and that she lived in an area with a "good view" of the many preternaturals living around here.

Those details may not have sounded like much to some, but they gave me a good starting point because it meant that she was almost certainly living on the outskirts of town. The largest tracts of forest were naturally away from our (admittedly small) 'downtown' area. A lot of the humans, both 'regular' and human psychics, lived in the downtown areas and in the apartment buildings, while a lot of the vampires and shapeshifters had migrated to living in the outskirts. I suspected that was something of the "good view" of the preternaturals, even for rural homes.

I went home and headed straight to my computer. Buster was asleep on my bed and barely seemed to notice I was there, which suited me just fine because I had work to do.

One of the handy things I was granted access to

for my work as a bounty hunter was a sort of 'behind the scenes' access to realtor listings. Bad guys like to hide in all sorts of places, and houses for sale could be good spots to choose. In this case, I needed to access ones that had been bought or were being rented in the past two years that also met all the other criteria I had determined. I suspected it was more likely she was renting under an assumed name, both to remain mobile and slightly more anonymous than getting a mortgage or paying for a house in cash would make her.

Unfortunately, there had been a fair amount of migration in and out of the city in the past few years, so the list of houses to check was not a small one.

Embarrassingly, everything caught up to me all at once, and I fell asleep while I was working...

Chapter Eighteen

I woke up to the ringing of a telephone.

My cell was buzzing obnoxiously, and I groggily reached for it. Squinting one eye, I checked the number but didn't recognize it offhand. Still, business calls weren't always ones that were in my contacts, so I answered it anyway.

"Hello?" I asked grumpily.

"It's the Adelheid PD lab," the voice on the other end replied immediately. This must have been someone who'd met me before because they didn't bother with any useless small talk. "We were able to get a match from that shirt you brought in yesterday."

That woke me up in an instant, and I sat up straight. "Yes?"

"Her name is Gia DeLuca. She wasn't born in Adelheid, but she was in the national database. I did a quick search on the name and can't find much on her, really. She fell off the radar over a decade ago, but there's an arrest from when she was eighteen, and that's how she ended up in the system."

Gia DeLuca... I felt like that name should mean something to me, given what she was, but it didn't.

"What was she arrested for?"

"Stalking," the other woman replied. "The charges were eventually dropped, but she apparently was harassing someone. It doesn't say what her reason was or why the charges were dropped. Do you want me to keep looking into it?"

"If you can," I said, a little distracted. "Be sure to tell Sam— I mean, Detective Moore about this." It was too early for Vance to be awake.

"Of course."

We hung up.

I meandered my way into the kitchen as my brain cells all played catchup with one another. Caffeine was in order, so I made some coffee and then returned to my room. When I sat back down at my computer, I saw the search window and the entry at the bottom of the list.

As I looked closer and clicked on it for more information, I realized that I had managed to fall asleep right as I'd found what I was looking for.

It was a small one-bedroom ranch on the outskirts of town with a lot of woodland around it. It had been rented by a woman named...right...Gina Luke twenty-two months ago. The reference for the lease application? Gino Lucas.

All the puzzle pieces were coming together.

I did something kind of stupid at that point, although I knew it was stupid when I chose to do it, to be fair. Really, I usually knew when I was doing dumbassery; I just chose to do it anyway.

The stupid thing I was doing at that moment was to go to the house I dug up on the real estate site without letting anyone know I was doing it. Should I have told Sam? Yes. Did I? No. I just hopped in my car and drove across town. On the upside, it wasn't one of the very rare gated communities in the area, so I didn't have to sneak in. That would probably have drawn too much attention to her desire to lay low, since such communities had particularly bitchy homeowners' associations and rules and fees and all that bullshit.

This was much more private and secluded. I debated whether I should park the car elsewhere and then approach in some kind of animal form, but I wasn't sure how astute her own senses were to me now...if she was even at the house in the first place. I had to hope she was. It wasn't the easiest place to track down, so it wasn't like anyone else was likely to find it. If I had to place a bet, I'd say she was there and getting ready to hop town.

It's what I would be doing, if I had been her.

I chose the more direct approach and just drove up to the house. There was one car in the driveway. It was a nice one, although not particularly ostentatious. It befitted the amount of money she was undoubtedly making without doing too much to draw attention to her. Hide in plain sight and all that. I placed my somewhat beat-up SUV beside it. (I could afford a new car, but I usually put cars through hell while on the job, so I didn't push my luck with that any more often than I had to.)

As I got out, I could see a window almost directly ahead of me. I smirked. There was a body moving beyond the semi-sheer curtains, and they were moving around very quickly.

"Someone is in a hurry," I whispered to myself.

I stood there for a moment, wondering if they would notice me in return, but apparently their urgency prevented them from catching me out quite so easily. I allowed that to give me a moment to determine how I wanted to go about this.

After a moment, I cast the single winning vote for the most direct route...

...and I threw myself through the window.

Broken glass littered the carpeted bedroom floor all around me as I rose to my feet and shook myself off. The woman I had been hoping to find here just stood, eyes wide and body frozen, staring at me.

"Hi, Gia," I said with a malicious smile.

She gaped a little like a fish for a moment as her brain tried to process the abrupt change in her circumstances. There was an open suitcase on the bed, and it was half-full. There was another bag open on top of the dresser, and that looked like it had a big ole pile of cash in it.

"It seems I got here just in time..." I went on, immediately advancing on her with all the stalking energy of the mountain lion shrieking in the back of my head. "You might have surprised me before, but no one catches me out like that twice. Certainly not the likes of you." I flashed my teeth. "I'm bigger, stronger, faster, and just all around better."

This seemed to pull her out of her shock and into anger instead. "Why, cause you're a pure blood?" she sneered.

I paused and tilted my head like a cat. "Well. *Yeah*. That, and I'm not evil incarnate."

"Bitch," she hissed, reeling back. I was sure she was about to shapeshift, but, again, I was faster...

I pulled my gun—yes, I had a permit for it and everything—and shot her in the leg.

The bullet was threaded with silver, which would hurt like hell against both the preternatural and not-preternatural sides of her being, and it would also hamper her ability to shift while it was in her body.

She spat curses of a creative nature, clearly offended that I had robbed her of another shapeshifting throwdown. With that off the table, she spun around clumsily and started to run away. Blood was already dripping on to the carpet after she'd made it one step, and I sighed and put my gun back in its holster. I wondered why people just couldn't accept defeat with grace...

She was almost to the door, but I had already changed into my beloved mountain lion form. I was across the room in the time it took her to grab the door handle, and my full body weight collided with her back. It smacked her face into the wood, and then we slid to the floor together. Once she was pinned, I shifted back to my human body and held her down. I pulled out my magic zip ties and hauled her hands together before I snagged some fabric something from a drawer and wrapped it around her wound.

I wanted her incapacitated, not dead.

Twisting her head to look back at me, she spat blood from where the collision with the floor had split her lip open. "You just think you're so great," she growled bitterly. She was understandably mad. I had stymied her escape and robbed her of some sort of epic climax scene, instead replacing it with something...far less exciting for her and much easier for myself.

"Sometimes, yeah," I replied with a verbal shrug, yanking the bandage tight and making her curse again. "And you, Ms. DeLuca, are not. You made a grave mistake when you brought your bullshit to my town."

Chapter Nineteen

Sam and I sat at my kitchen table with about fifteen different file folders open and covering it, various pieces of paper scattered all on top of them alongside three different notebooks covered in her scrawled handwriting.

"You were right about the shell companies," she said, tapping one of the pads with her pen. "We are still digging them up and tracing through the epic maze she created. This was masterful manipulation, and I think we may still be uncovering things years from now. She is, obviously, not giving us any help. Plenty of vitriol for both sides of her heritage and how they equally ruined her life somehow but not much else."

My girlfriend had been kind enough, and restrained enough, to keep any thoughts about my snagging DeLuca solo to herself. After all, really, this was basically my job. I almost never had help when I was tracking down some pretty dangerous folks, and DeLuca's real danger was in her brilliance combined with the depth of her depravity. One-on-one, she wasn't much of a threat to me once she didn't have the advantage of a huge fucking surprise.

"We have gotten to all of the locations referenced in the files we found and cleared them out of their victims. We've returned bodies to the families we've been able to find, and we're still looking for the rest." She sighed heavily. "I don't know how many of them are going to make it through this in any sort of okay state. Most of them, if they even survived it, are looking at a very long road to healing."

"Nykk is the person to guide that effort," I said, taking Sam's hand and squeezing it slightly because I could tell she was bothered. "She's walked that long road to healing personal trauma, after all."

Sam nodded and didn't linger on it. "If you recall Pre-Tech, the company that tried to make the super preternatural that just turned into a rampant killing machine?"

How could I forget...

"I've seen some references to that company too, although in that case, I think she was working with a legitimate company rather than Pre-Tech being one of her businesses."

"I don't know if that makes me feel better or worse," I commented.

She made a small grunt of agreement. "I don't know, either, but I can't say I like it. It might not mean much of anything, ultimately, but we'll keep digging into it. Just to be sure." She shuffled through the papers. "A hotshot lawyer from Boston has already driven down to start representing DeLuca," she continued, "and I'm sure he will have something to say about the fact you shot her."

I shrugged. "Let him pitch a fit. I was apprehending

a dangerous suspect who was in the process of fleeing the jurisdiction and who had already used violence against me in a previous encounter. I was within the rights of my job."

It wasn't like I hadn't been through this a time or two. You always did, in my line of work.

She smiled at me and squeezed my hand. "I'm sure he's no match for you."

That made me laugh. "There's only one person who can take me down."

"Oh?" She raised her brows.

I raised my brows and said nothing.

Our little stare-down didn't last long, however, because Edward and Lorelei walked in. We relented simultaneously and turned to them. Buster managed to drag himself out of napping in the bedroom and lazily walked up to us. I absently dropped my hand to scratch the top of his head before I even realized I had done it. It was funny how well dogs could train us. Until this goofy bastard, I had never imagined myself as a dog person, but here we were...

"Still working?" Edward asked as he shut the door behind him.

"We're just wrapping up," I said, turning to the table and stopping with the dog-pats to collect papers into folders so Edward and Lorelei didn't have to see any of this. They knew about the things going on with Sam and I, what our jobs were and what they entailed, but I still didn't think they needed to know the grisly details. They had their lives going just fine without it and while I could be a bitch most of the time, I did love my family and valued their peace as much as I could.

After we straightened everything up and got it out of sight, the four of us moved into the living room. I couldn't help but notice that Lorelei's pregnancy was already showing, and she moved like it was affecting her gait. Even her smell was changing, which was really weird. I realized that I hadn't spent much time around pregnant people, especially this up close and regularly, so I hadn't noticed that before...or maybe it was the nature of the baby she was carrying? I couldn't know for sure either way.

"How are you feeling?" Sam asked with a smile as she leaned against me, almost a silent reminder that she could be happy for my brother's growing family without having the urge for her own.

"I'm good," Lorelei replied, "but so tired. I've read up about the first trimester, but I feel like I'm already into my second." She gestured down at her burgeoning midsection. "I look like I am too, and I know it, so you don't have to keep it to yourself." This was directed at me with a smirk, but it was a loving one so I was okay with being teased.

I looked at my brother. "Do you think having a half-theriomorph baby will make the pregnancy different?"

He shrugged helplessly. "How should I know?"

"Were either of you old enough to see one of your mother's pregnancies?" Sam asked. I knew she was in the middle of her own pack, but their ages were close enough together that she didn't remember much. Still, she didn't need to. Pure human pregnancies were pretty well mapped out.

Edward and I exchanged a look. Had we both somehow managed to neglect this family detail? "We were actually all the same age, kind of like a litter."

"A litter?!" Lorelei exclaimed with a look of panic in her dark eyes. "Excuse me? What?!"

He immediately grabbed her hand and kissed the back of it. "Both of our parents were theriomorphs, so however it went for them isn't how it will be for us," he assured her. I couldn't really say she looked all that reassured, however. "And we'll get an ultrasound and find out. I'm sure there aren't six babies in there, though."

The poor woman still looked alarmed. "There better not be," she murmured. "I don't think I could handle that." She looked down at her waist, and her brows knit. "I think we should talk to that doctor about the ultrasound sooner than expected."

"Why?" This question came from all three of us, all concerned at the sudden turn in her expression and suggestion.

"The baby just kicked," she said, mouth dropping open as she lifted her head and looked between us. "I felt a kick already!"

No one knew what to say about that, so we all just looked at one another with the same open-mouthed confusion. "I mean, maybe theriomorph babies just develop really fast," Sam said. "Even half-theriomorphs."

If DeLuca wasn't a total sadistic, evil bitch, I could have asked her... I didn't mention that now, however. "Nurse Ciara in town is also a midwife and specializes with preternatural species," I said. "I'm sure if you call and explain your situation, she'll get you in for an appointment as soon as possible."

Edward already had his phone out, looking up the nurse who'd set her practice up in downtown Adelheid. Her office wasn't far from the Stanton Agency, actually. While he did that, I was seized by an impulse that was totally unlike me, but...I gestured toward Lorelei's stomach. "May I?" The question came out with a lot more uncertainty than I liked in my tone.

That made her smile a little. "Sure," she said, moving her hands away.

Almost nervously, I moved off the couch and knelt next to her armchair. I tentatively put my hand on her stomach, almost as if afraid I'd hurt her or the baby just by...being me. She moved my hand slightly, and after a moment, I felt the small push against her skin.

"What the fuck!" I exclaimed, unable to help myself, and then we all laughed.

"I think that about sums it up," Lorelei said with a wry smile, "from start to finish. We're not naming the kid that, though."

After dinner, Sam and I took Buster for a walk. We stuck closer to the property than I often had in the past, but he was still limping very slightly, and I was still having small flashbacks to those people trying to abduct us. He didn't mind where we went, however. He just liked being outside and he liked being with us. I liked being outside too, given how much of my life I had spent living in the woods.

"Your life is about to get a whole lot more interesting," Sam teased me, "and a lot sooner than you expected."

"I'm sure they won't expect me to do much with the baby." I smirked. "They know I tend to scare children."

She nudged me in the ribs. "You're not gonna scare this one. I'm certain of it. He, or she, will know that you're family, and I bet you'll even enjoy having a little niece or nephew. Honestly, being an aunt is fun. You can take the kids and do silly things, stuff them with sugar and give them back to their folks."

I looked sidelong at her and laughed. "You do that to your siblings, do you?"

"Of course," she replied without hesitation. "My oldest brother used to swap the salt and sugar before I put what I thought was sugar on my toast. And one of my sisters used to hide my dolls on high shelves. Frankly, they have it coming."

"That's hard to argue with, then," I agreed.

I hadn't actually met any of her family, but they lived in the Boston suburbs and weren't as close at hand as my very small family here in Adelheid was. She didn't even see them often, given how busy her job kept her. Maybe I would meet them someday, but I didn't push.

My mind meandered for a little while as our path around the edges of the property also meandered. "I wonder if we'll ever know more about the mystery of that DeLuca woman," I commented. "Where did she come from? What's her story, beyond hating purebloods and hating being half-preternatural?

What happened to her, and are we related?"

Sam squeezed my hand. "I hope we can find some answers for you, but she's hardly going to be forthcoming. She is smart but also savage."

"Sadistic," I added, since we were coming up with S words.

"That too." She paused. "I can't say I'm not worried she'll find a way to get out. You don't do all that she did, build all that she did, without being very clever. Either her lawyer will pull some kind of trick, or she'll find some way to escape..."

That thought had occurred to me too, of course, but I had a simple answer to it. "If she gets out, then I'll just do what I do best and hunt her ass down again."

About the Author

Born a Connecticut Yankee in nobody's court, K. B. Thorne grew up to brave snow and talk fast.

She started reading when she was three and never looked back, soon frequently falling asleep with a book under her cheek. At eleven, she discovered *Night Mare* by Piers Anthony and entered the world of grown-up fantasy fiction. As you can guess, it was all over from there. She started writing at fourteen, then met vampires as a teenager and the concept for what would become Adelheid (now the Blood Rights Series) was soon born. Mia Darien followed a few years later, and the books were released.

However, K. B. is also a third-generation Trekkie. Somewhere in a vault at Paramount is a very angry letter written by her grandmother when *Star Trek: The Original Series* was cancelled, so sci-fi is in the blood too. Alongside a love of love, and an adoration for her first love of epic fantasy.

K. B. Thorne is the evolution of Mia Darien after years of learning and living. She has taken both of those things to become a smarter, better writer with a fresh new face and take on the literary world. Thorne writes the urban fantasy, fantasy and sci-fi, while Sadie Johnston writes the romance.

These days, when she's not desperately trying to find time to write, she works as a freelance editor/cover artist/formatter and happily lives her unconventional life alongside her very own Named Man of the North and their mini-tank. (Who is, you know, their son.)

You can find more at authorkbthorne.com.

Other Books
by K. B. Thorne

Writing as K. B. Thorne
Blood Rights Series

Bad Blood
Blood and Thunder
Blood Moon
Written in Blood
Bloodshot
First Blood
Out for Blood
New Blood
Flesh and Blood

Bellator (Anthology)
Good Things (Anthology)
Ashes to Sunrise (Anthology)
The Shape of Tomorrow (Anthology)
Born of Defiance (Anthology)

Writing as Sadie Johnston (Romance)
Beauty
Help Wanted (with Viola Dawn)
Threnody (with Alastair Malone)
Here, Kitty Kitty (Anthology)
Amor Vincit Omnia (Anthology)
Second Chances (Anthology)